# ARCTIC GAUNTLET

## D.J. GOODMAN

SEVERED PRESS
HOBART TASMANIA

# ARCTIC GAUNTLET

Sometimes horrible and strange things happen without reason. People can debate for years afterward what caused it, and might even come close to some semblance of the truth, but they will never know for certain. What's about to happen in the Arctic is just such a case, and no one in the world will ever have definite answers.

But if you are the kind that absolutely will not be satisfied without some clue as to the greater scheme, then know this:

There are certain places throughout the world, places that have been set up in secret. Interested parties might be able to find a map of these places elsewhere, but for our purposes most of them don't matter. One, however, does.

Somewhere in the Arctic Circle, deep below water that most humans wouldn't be able to survive in thanks to the cold, and formerly under a patch of ice that has only recently melted away after existing for untold years, there is a box. Perhaps "box" is not the right word for it. That might imply something small, something made of cardboard that your Amazon order comes in. No, this is large, not that anyone will ever see it to describe its specific size. After today, the various mechanisms that keep it suspended in the deep will fail and this cube will sink, vanishing in the darkness to rot for an unknown number of years.

This you can guess about the size, though: it's large enough to comfortably house four things. Four very large things, in fact. The top and the bottom of the cube are featureless, but the remaining four sides each have a door. The doors have large, faded numbers on the outside, the paint stripped away to almost nothing, but still faintly readable at this time. On one side of door number one, there is a tiny puff of air and water as a small explosive device goes off, releasing the door's lock.

*Door number one does not immediately swing open. Instead the thing inside continues to swim around in its confines, completely unaware that it is now free.*

*As we wait for the thing behind door number one, door number two experiences a similar change. Unlike number one, though, the currents pull the door open slightly, allowing the thing inside to realize it's free. Still, there is a moment of hesitation, as though the occupant thinks this might be a trick. Then it nudges at the door, finds that the door is no longer barred against it, and tentatively heads out into the open ocean.*

*The noises from the room next to it finally alert the occupant of door number one that something has changed. Rather than carefully check to see if it can escape, this one slams directly into the door, as if trying to punish it for the occupant's incarceration. This gives the thing behind door number one a particularly explosive exit, and even if anyone were around to witness all this, the creature behind door number one would be gone before anyone could see it and describe it. Like its neighbor behind door number two, this one vanishes into the deep blue.*

*The lock blows on door number three. This time the door opens with no hesitation at all, as though its occupant had been aware this was going to happen. It leaves with slow but intentional purpose. It knows that two others came before it. It knows that they will prepare its way. It knows that when it joins the others, they will all have much sport.*

*The fourth and final door does not open.*

*From inside, something smashes against the door. Any observer, if such a person hadn't already left out of terror at the sights that came out of the first three doors, might interpret the deep, heavy thuds of the last occupant as angry, like perhaps it knows the others have gone. Maybe it is even smart enough to realize that, whatever force there might have been that put these four creatures in the box, this force knew that the last one must never be unleashed, that whatever horror and chaos the first three might release on the world, the unimaginable terror of the fourth was too much even for their standards.*

*Something smashes at the door again. A visible dent appears. Another will appear soon. And another. Door number four will not hold out for much longer. The door will fail, and the occupant will escape.*

*You do not want to be here when it does. You will be some distance away, watching events unfold, but you will know this is happening. You will know something is coming. You will know that the events you're going to watch will be catastrophic.*

*But before you go, one last detail. Upon closer inspection, you see that the top of the box is not as featureless as you first thought. Much like the numbers on the doors, there is something painted here that has lost most of it definition in the frozen elements. It's not a number, though. It's some kind of curving, twisting shape in silver and blue.*

*Is that supposed to be a paperclip? You think it might be, but that doesn't make any sense. What would a paperclip have to do with any of this?*

*This is not a question you will have answered, at least not just now. Perhaps if you search in the right places, the right stories, at some point in the future you might eventually know.*

*But for now that is enough. You have other events you need to witness.*

*And then, sometime very soon, you will have carnage.*

# CHAPTER ONE

Quinne gripped the cold metal of the railing, closed her eyes, and took a deep breath through her nose. The scent of salt water assaulted her nostrils, along with something else. She knew this scent, had in fact grown up with it as a young girl living in small-town Minnesota, yet she had no name for it. No one did, as far as she was aware. People who had never lived in colder climates wouldn't even know that there was a scent for this. Except it wasn't really a scent at all. It was more like the absence of a scent. The hairs in one's nostrils, or whatever the hell it might be that sensed odors, felt like they froze in the cold. It was the smell of frozen wind, icy tundra, and air dry from the moisture hardening before it could permeate the air.

To most people, this wouldn't be their definition of perfect vacation weather. To Quinne Quiver, it was heaven.

Not that anyone here on the cruise ship would officially know her by that name. Her ticket, her credit card, her passport, were all under her legal name, Laurie Schnellmann. She still kept that name for all her mundane needs, but that wasn't how she thought of herself, and when she was in company that she thought would be receptive, she introduced herself as Quinne. Sometimes people would recognize the name, but most of the people who might be familiar with her wouldn't truly recognize her with her clothes on.

And her clothes were definitely going to be on for the majority of this trip. This was day three of the *Lucky Lady Duck*'s ten-day cruise of the Arctic, and even though it was in the middle of summer, that didn't matter this far north. Even with massive amounts of ice melting, this was still one of the colder parts of the planet. Any time she went outside, she would need her heavy coat and gloves. The bulky winter-wear covered up her lanky form and massive number of tattoos. The only hints of her trademark style that were still visible were her midnight black hair and dark makeup. It set her apart from most of the other passengers on what was typically known as a squeaky-clean cruise liner. Parents kept their children away from her, and although a few single guys had made passes at her, there was still something intimidating about her manner that kept all but the boldest away.

Which was actually kind of a problem right now, since night was starting to fall and Quinne had gone for almost a whole week without sex. She was really horny about now.

She supposed she could go and find one of the many bars in the *Lucky Lady Duck*'s mall-like corridors and get herself a companion for the night, but for now the view on deck was a more powerful lure than her libido. Most of the passengers had gone in for dinner, leaving Quinne alone with this amazing sunset—which, she had to remind herself, wasn't actually a sunset at all. According to their itinerary, the sun would actually begin setting again in the final days of their trip, but then only for extremely brief periods of time before it rose again. During summer in the Arctic, there were days so long they technically didn't end at all. It provided a view at all hours of the day, and just the day before, Quinne had taken advantage of this, coming out in what was supposed to be the small hours of the morning and getting an amazing view all to herself of whales breaching in the middle distance. If she were lucky, she might see something again if she were only patient enough.

Her ears picked up something very quiet from behind her, and she knew she was no longer alone. She stiffened, but wouldn't turn around. Old habits would dictate that she immediately be on alert, especially since she was effectively alone with whoever this might be. But she'd worked very hard not to let such small things set her on edge. Not everything was an impending disaster, and not every random person was going to attack her.

Still, there were enough of her old habits left that she carefully listened to the person's every tiny movement, tracking them as they walked around behind her. Her best guess was that the person was female, and probably rather small, maybe even smaller than Quinne's petite frame. Whoever it was, she was practiced at being quiet, unobtrusive. Someone timid, maybe. Quinne knew what it was like to be like that. She worked hard to do the opposite now. Timidity wasn't exactly an asset in her line of work.

Quinne didn't turn to look at the person as she took a position at the railing farther down the deck, but after several seconds she made a quick glance in her direction. She was right that it had been a woman, although maybe girl would have been more accurate. At twenty, many people considered Quinne practically a baby herself, but this one was young enough that Quinne couldn't actually be sure if she was an adult or not. She also had a significant difference in the way she dressed. Oh, she was in all the proper outerwear for the weather, but she also wore a hijab. In fact, Quinne thought she might have seen the young woman around on the ship. She'd also seen random assholes whisper behind the girl's back when she wasn't looking. The girl had appeared to be travelling alone, which probably only gave the shithead gossips more fuel to work with.

Quinne pulled out a cigarette and lighter from her coat pocket. The *Lucky Lady Duck* was supposed to be strictly smoke-free, but in just a few days Quinne had grown quite adept at sneaking in her habit while no one was looking.

"Hey," Quinne said. "Want a smoke?"

The girl jerked around to look at her, like Quinne had suddenly appeared next to her out of nowhere. "What?" the girl asked.

"A smoke," Quinne said, holding the cigarette up. "Want a cigarette?"

"Um, no. Thank you. I don't smoke."

"Well, I'm going to smoke. If it bothers you, just let me know and I can find a place somewhere else on the deck."

"I'm pretty sure that's not supposed to be allowed."

"And I'm pretty sure you're right." Quinne stuck the filter in her mouth and lit the cigarette. She took a deep drag, then angled the smoke out the side of her mouth so she wasn't blowing it directly in the girl's face. She thought for a second that the girl would indeed ask her to move, and if she did Quinne would do it with no problem. Smoking was a rather new habit for her, something she had taken up almost by accident in order to pass the down time when she was waiting on yet another flaky male talent to show up at the set. Having watched her mother die of lung cancer, she was very much aware of why others might not want anything to do with smokers. But she knew others who did a lot worse than just smoke, so she figured she was doing pretty good.

The girl didn't say anything, though. She didn't even take a step away from Quinne. In fact, she leaned forward just a bit. After several seconds the girl said, "Actually, can I try one after all?"

Quinne raised an eyebrow but said nothing as she pulled her pack back out of her pocket and shook another one out. She handed the girl both the cigarette and the lighter, but she looked at them both as though she didn't have the first clue how to start. Quinne pocketed the lighter again, then lit the second cigarette on her own and handed it to her.

"Thanks," the girl said. The cigarette looked awkward in her hand, like she'd never held one before, and Quinne fully expected her to erupt in coughs when she took her first drag. She didn't, though. The girl held the smoke in her lungs for several seconds before letting it out. "Kind of burns, doesn't it?"

"It can," Quinne said. "I'm Quinne, by the way."

The girl gave her a long, appraising look, the kind that people clearly gave Quinne when they felt a spark of recognition and were trying to picture her butt naked just to be sure. Quinne cocked an eyebrow again. Maybe she wasn't as much the innocent as she had first appeared.

"Amani," she replied.

"Pleased to meet you, Amani."

Amani took one more drag, then handed the cigarette back. "That's all I really needed for now. Thanks."

Quinne nodded, pinched off the ash, and then put the rest of the partially smoked cigarette back in the pack. "I take it that's not usual for you?"

"No, it's just... You just looked... I don't know. So calm smoking it."

"Needed some calming down?"

"Yeah, I guess I did."

"And did it work?"

"I don't know. Maybe." But Quinne could tell that there was no maybe about it. All of the quietness and hesitancy she'd seen when Amani approached was gone now.

"Want to talk about it?" Quinne asked.

"No."

Quinne nodded, then turned back to look out at the icy open ocean. She couldn't help but notice the way Amani stood closer to her now, just outside Quinne's personal bubble.

After several minutes of silence, Amani spoke again. "You here with anyone?"

"I'm with you, ain't I?"

"I mean here on the cruise. On the ship."

"Nope. Just me. Personal vacation. What about you? You alone?"

Amani tensed. "Yes. Is that a problem?"

"Why would that be a problem?"

"People see someone like me, with my clothing and my colored skin, and then they find out that I'm travelling alone, they start to back away from me. You know, or start to report my every move to ship security."

"Seriously?" Quinne asked. "Man, fuck people. People suck."

Amani smiled.

There were several more moments of silence where Quinne thought out her next actions. There would be nothing wrong with it, she decided, as long as she was respectful if Amani wasn't interested.

"Amani, are you eighteen?"

Amani frowned. "That's kind of an odd question."

"Well, I know you recognized me. Technically, most people shouldn't recognize me if they're not legally an adult."

Amani looked away, clearly embarrassed. "I'm sorry."

"What's to be sorry for?"

"For staring. It's not every day someone meets a… you know."

"You can say it. The words won't bite you."

"A porn star."

"Actually, I would say that I meet other porn stars quite often. But that's kind of beside the point. You still didn't answer the question."

"Eighteen isn't the technical age for adulthood everywhere, you know."

"I know. But just because we're in international waters doesn't mean long-trained habits on my part just go away."

"Okay. Yes, I'm eighteen. I still think that's an odd question."

"I asked because I don't invite anyone back to my room if they're not eighteen," Quinne said.

Amani did a double take at her. If she'd been drinking something, Quinne was sure it would have sprayed out of her mouth and into the Arctic Ocean.

"If you're not interested, that's cool," Quinne said. "You don't need to feel awkward about saying no."

"Do you often ask total strangers to sleep with you?"

"I wouldn't say often. But I'm not afraid of looking for what I want, either."

"Oh. Well, uh, I'm not..."

"Gotcha. No worries. I just thought that if you recognized me, it would be more likely from my girl-girl work."

Amani was silent for a long time. Finally she said, "Actually, that is where I recognize you from."

Quinne nodded. "Not something you're used to admitting to strangers, is it?"

Amani went quiet again. Quinne knew exactly what she was seeing. Hell, she'd had to go through this once herself. Amani here was a baby gay. She was still trying to come to terms with whatever she might be, whether it was lesbian or bisexual. She was curious, she knew what she wanted to do and try, but she was scared. Maybe she had family that wouldn't approve. That might account for why the girl was on a trip like this alone. This was about soul searching. Of course, when Quinne had needed to come to terms with being pansexual, her own searching had been in the backs of pickups rather than on a family cruise liner.

"Look, if you're not ready or you're just not interested in me in particular, that's okay. Trust me on this: you don't want to push it. But if you do change your mind, I'm sure you'll see me around the ship."

Quinne stubbed out her cigarette, tucked away the filter where she could later properly throw it away rather than chucking it in the ocean, and started to head back inside. She wasn't terribly surprised, though, when Amani caught her by the arm.

"Wait. Maybe... maybe we could just go back... I mean, head to your room and... well, you know."

"Just see what happens?" Quinne asked with a smile.

"Yeah." Amani's voice was quiet, almost reverential, like she thought this was going to be some huge, unforgettable moment in her life. Quinne made a mental note, if this did go all the way tonight, to do what she could to make it memorable for her.

"Okay then," Quinne said. "If you're ready to go back…" Her voice trailed off as she saw something in the distance. "Wait. Look!"

Amani turned to the ocean. "I don't know what I'm supposed to be looking at."

"Over in that direction," Quinne said, pointing. "On the water. Just wait a second…"

It took more than a second, but they were rewarded for their patience. A whale breached and splashed back down in the water. It hadn't come up very far, but their brief glimpse of it was beautiful. Quinne didn't know enough to be able to guess what species it might be, other than it was definitely something other than an orca and definitely large. Sperm whale maybe? Or a humpback? She couldn't tell the difference, nor did she really care. After a few more seconds other whales could be seen at the surface, none of them showing themselves as spectacularly as the first but all equally breathtaking. Several of them spit plumes of water high into the air from their blowholes.

"Wow," Amani said quietly. "I've heard other people saying they've seen whales on this trip, but this is a first for me."

As they watched in reverent silence, Amani moved closer to her and, for an awkward second, looked like she was considering whether or not to take Quinne's hand. The gesture was usually a bit too twee for Quinne, but she reached out and took Amani's hand herself. This would likely be a night the girl would remember for the rest of her life, after all. Quinne didn't see why she shouldn't make it nice for her.

Amani's hand gripped hers harder. At first Quinne thought it was some kind of cutesy gesture of affection or thanks, but when Amani pointed at the whale with her other hand, the look on her face was distinctly worried. "Um, are they supposed to be doing that?"

Quinne squinted at the whales. They seemed to be thrashing in the water more than usual, churning up a large amount of mist that made it harder to see them. "I don't know," Quinne said.

There was a flume of water, then another. Every spray after that was not water at all, but blood.

# CHAPTER TWO

"Dafuq?" Quinne asked.

"Okay, that I know for sure isn't supposed to happen," Amani said.

"Yeah, I think you're right." Quinne kept staring, thinking maybe she wasn't seeing blood at all. It could have just been a trick of the light. With the sun rather close to the horizon, it was entirely possible that what they saw was just an illusion. But no. As the water churned faster, more and more of it was clearly tinted pink.

"Wow," Amani said. "Are they being attacked by, like, killer whales?"

Quinne shrugged. Her knowledge of killer whales began and ended with the bits and pieces she'd caught of *Blackfish* once as it was playing in the background while she made out with some guy she'd picked up. Hardly a doctorate course in marine biology. "Would a killer whale even attack another whale?"

"I don't know," Amani said.

Quinne wanted to turn away, but she was held rapt by the blood bath. She took a quick look up and down the deck to see if anyone else was witnessing this, but the deck was quiet. It was dinner time, after all. The few random people that were out for now were engrossed in their own activities: a family of four where both parents were trying to calm down their crying toddler, an older couple walking hand in hand, a middle-aged woman facing away from the ocean with a cell phone in one ear and her finger in the other as she tried to get a signal. Quinne and Amani appeared to be the only people noticing the strange display in the distance.

"Do you have a cell phone to record this?" Quinne asked Amani.

"It's back in my cabin. You?"

"Intentionally left mine at home. The whole point of going on vacation is to get some time away from my normal world."

The spray of blood stopped. The water became calm for a second. Try as she might, Quinne couldn't see any more sign of the whales. Either they had all taken evasive maneuvers against their predator, or else they were all dead.

"That's really weird," Amani said. "It's so peaceful out there all of a sudden."

"Nature can be a scary bitch," Quinne said, but despite her flippant words, she was uneasy. She continued staring out at the water, looking for any sign of what had really happened. The water began to churn again, but this time the disturbance was closer by about half the distance. It looked like something moving through the water, heading directly for the *Lucky Lady Duck*. The closer it got, the more obvious it became that whatever it was, it was big. Bigger, possibly, than any of the whales had been.

Then whatever it was dove and vanished completely from all sight.

"Do you think we should tell someone about this?" Amani asked.

"Maybe. But what are we supposed to say? Something ate a bunch of whales, then came at the ship but then changed its mind? Even if anyone believes us, they would probably say that it was exactly what we first thought. Orcas, or something else like that."

"Quinne, I really don't think that was an orca."

"No, I don't think so either." Quinne paused and thought for a few seconds. "Let's just go see if anyone would pay any attention. If not, and they don't think it's a big deal, then maybe it isn't.

Maybe we can just get on back to my room like we were planning. Assuming you still want that?"

It was Amani's turn to pause. "Yes. I still think I would."

# CHAPTER THREE

The two of them ended up being both right and wrong. They were wrong that they were the only people who had noticed anything worrying. But they were right that the majority of people wouldn't believe it.

Inside the ship, in the main rotunda, Quinne and Amani saw a small crowd gathering near the elevators. Several of them were obviously members of the crew, given their immaculate white uniforms, and Quinne thought she vaguely recognized one man as the captain himself. Facing the crew were three men, and around the two groups there was a circle of onlookers. Quinne pushed through the crowd to get a closer look at the men, making sure that no one jostled Amani behind her. Quinne nearly took a step back when she saw them, although it was Amani who actually gave voice to her thoughts.

"Holy cow, is someone filming an action movie here?"

Because that was exactly what the three men looked like: the lead cast in the latest Hollywood summer blockbuster. The one who stood in front of the others, with his arms crossed in a pose that clearly said "I'm the leader and you're going to listen to me," had pale skin and a shock of red hair, but neither feature was as striking as his enormous muscles. He could have easily been a wrestler or a body builder. The man behind him and to his right was equally good looking, if not as insanely well-built. His skin had an indeterminate brown color, like the unthreatening "maybe ethnic or maybe just ambiguously tanned" look of so many action movie sidekicks. The third man was definitely white, the color of someone who rarely went out into the sun, and he had the stringy build and wild hair of the designated nerd of the group. But it was a Los Angeles type of geekiness, like the appearance was more of an affectation than an actual way of life for him.

When the first guy spoke, he did so with the tone of some former athlete acting for the first time and not knowing how to properly read his lines.

"It is true. Mickey's readings do not lie."

The captain responded as though they had been having this conversation for a while now, and he was completely ready to be done with it. "Look, Mr. Masterson…"

"It's Doctor Masterson. I have a PhD in science."

Quinne raised an eyebrow but kept her mouth shut.

"Fine. Doctor. We have plenty of equipment constantly monitoring the surrounding waters for anything large and out of the ordinary like an iceberg. If anything came close to the ship that was larger than a small boat, we would know. And I haven't been informed of any such thing."

"Captain, we know what our sensors picked up," the second man said. His tone wasn't anywhere near as stilted at Masterson's. He even had an air of actual competence about him. "There is something very large out there, and it came directly for the ship before diving. You've got to get the word out to someone that can help. I think every single man, woman, and child on this ship is in danger."

"What kind of sensors are you even talking about?" the captain asked. "Is this even something you're supposed to have on the ship?"

"It's top secret," the third guy said. The way his eyes were dilated, Quinne would almost swear that he was stoned. "Very hush-hush, need to know, James Bond-type shit."

"Mickey, please shut up," Masterson said. "Look captain,

Mickey, Gordon, and I are all men of science. That means we're smart. We know what we're talking about. You must believe us or else we will all be in danger."

"Wow," Amani muttered under her breath. "Are these guys for real?"

"Probably not," Quinne whispered back. "What do you think? Should we speak up?"

"I'm not so sure that's a good idea anymore," Amani said. "If we didn't sound crazy before, we're definitely going to seem off our gourd after these guys."

"Dr. Masterson, you will refrain from causing any more trouble aboard my ship," the captain said. "If you persist in causing a ruckus, I shall be forced to have you and your two friends taken by security and escorted to the brig."

"Do cruise ships have brigs?" Quinne quietly asked Amani. Amani just shrugged.

"This is crazy. You will all regret this!" With that, Masterson turned and stalked off, although maybe that was the wrong word for it, as he only moved about ten feet. As if this were a cue to everyone else, the crowd broke up and went back to their business. The captain stayed behind to whisper some kind of instructions to his crew. One of the women who had been watching, a busty blonde, went over to Masterson and began speaking to him, her body language obviously flirty.

"That was surreal," Quinne said.

"Maybe we should go after them, tell them what we saw?" Amani asked.

Quinne was about to take her advice, except she saw a father break away from his family of five and go over to Masterson, saying just loud enough for her to hear that he had seen something. It sounded like, from wherever he had been, he might have had a better view than even Quinne and Amani.

"Probably won't be able to give any better information than

that guy. Besides, I don't think that's our story."

"Our story? What exactly do you think is 'our story'?"

"Well, since I don't think there's actually anything for us to worry about, our story right now revolves around whether or not you've changed your mind."

Amani took a long, deep breath. Quinne was certain she was about to say that anything between them would be a bad idea. If that's what came out of her mouth, then Quinne would accept it with no questions and they would go their separate ways. However, Quinne didn't think she would then go trolling any of the bars or hotspots on the ship. Suddenly, if she didn't spend the evening with this sweet, vulnerable girl, Quinne didn't think she would be in the mood to spend it with anyone else.

"Maybe... I could just go back to your room with you? No promises of anything else?"

Quinne smiled. "Sure. If that's what you want, I could make some coffee."

"Is that... are you talking about real coffee, or is this that thing where coffee actually means sex?"

"That's one hundred percent up to you. Personally, if all you want to do is chat for a while and then head on your way, I'll still consider it an evening well spent."

They made their way past several shops and small cafes, ignoring the elevators and stairs that led down to the entertainment level, where there were multiple theaters showing everything from movies to magic shows. Quinne had been surprised that one of the acts performing on the *Lucky Lady Duck* was Troid and Murga, the famous magic-and-wombat-act that had once been such a big hit in Vegas. Then an animal rights group had vehemently opposed their use of a rare, endangered species of wombat in the act, so they had needed to switch to using capybaras. Apparently capybaras weren't nearly as entertaining, because the illusionists had then faded into obscurity, and now it seemed cruise ships were the only place they could perform their act.

Amani glanced at the stairs and shrugged. "Have you ever been on a cruise ship before this?" she asked.

"No. Why?"

"It's just that from day one I've been a bit confused about the way the *Lucky Lady Duck* is laid out. If I didn't know any better, I would say it had been designed by someone who's never actually been on a cruise ship before."

"Yeah. I overheard one of the other passengers say it was as though the person who put it together was basing everything on poorly remembered scenes from *The Love Boat*."

"What's *The Love Boat*?"

"I don't know for sure, but I'm assuming it's a TV show so old that nobody important remembers it anymore."

"The entire ship is a bit more, uh, mall-like than I expected."

Quinne nodded. "That probably has more to do with the Letroix Corporation than anyone else. This is what happens when you make most of your money off family movies and then try to expand into the cruise market. It's basically their attempt to be Disneyland on the water."

"Which is why I thought it was kind of odd that you, of all people, would be here," Amani said. "Especially alone."

They had reached the corridor that led down to Quinne's rooms. On one side of the hall were a row of doors leading into the individual cabins and suites, while on the other side there was a number of portholes looking out over the ocean. The floors were some sort of immaculately polished material while the walls were decorated in faux-wood. This level was two below the main deck, making their view through the small windows much closer to the water.

"Why would you say that?" Quinne asked.

"You know. Family-friendly cruise line. Family-friendly ship. And here you are, uh…"

"Not family-friendly in the slightest?"

"Right."

"Ah, but that's exactly the point," Quinne said. "I like the fact that…"

She trailed off.

"What?" Amani asked. "Is something wrong?"

"I… I don't know," Quinne said. That wasn't true. Something was most definitely wrong, but she couldn't consciously figure out what it was just yet. They both stopped in the middle of the hall, at least five doors down from Quinne's room. "Did you just notice anything off just now?"

"No. I don't think so." Still, Amani turned around and looked up and down the hall. The two of them were alone in the immediate vicinity, but behind them there was an African-American couple pulling out the card key to go into their room while a lone little boy sat outside a door much farther down, his face immersed in a book. It all looked pretty normal.

Except for the light, Quinne realized. Something was wrong with the light. The corridor was lit with fluorescent lamps hanging above them, but they weren't the only source of illumination. The windows still let in a half-assed twilight from the perpetually setting, but never actually set, sun.

It was here that the anomaly showed itself. The light from outside dimmed, then grew brighter. Dimmed again, brighter again.

"Did you notice any clouds in the sky while we were on the deck?" Quinne asked.

"No. The sky was clear."

"Then where are the moving shadows outside coming from?"

That was when the entire ship shook with an impact.

# CHAPTER FOUR

All the people in the hall went completely quiet. The couple behind them had stopped their quiet giggling and stared up at the overhead lamps, which were swaying with the impact. The little boy had stood up, although he didn't seem to understand what had happened any more than anyone else. The door behind him opened to reveal a woman wearing nothing but a bed sheet. "What was that?" the woman asked. "Honey, are you alright?"

"Did we just hit something?" Amani asked Quinne. "An iceberg or something?"

"I don't know how we could," Quinne said. "This isn't the Titanic. They have equipment to monitor those things and avoid them now. At least, I think they do. Right?"

Before Amani could agree or disagree, there was a second shuddering blow. Unlike the first's origin, which Quinne hadn't been able to pinpoint, this one very clearly came from the outer wall up ahead.

She could tell this because two of the porthole windows exploded.

They were about fifteen feet down the hall from Quinne and Amani, close enough that Quinne thought she felt a subtle sharp spray of fine glass particles but far enough away that neither of them suffered any major lacerations. The boy screamed and wrapped his arms around the woman, who Quinne assumed was his mother, as a second person, a man, came out into the hallway as he pulled his boxer shorts on.

"Holy shit!" Quinne screamed.

"We should run!" Amina replied. And yet they both stood still, utterly petrified and mesmerized. Before anyone at all in the hallway could move, there was a third blow. And with it, the outer wall blew apart as a huge reptilian head, the size of the entire hallway, smashed in.

Multiple people in the corridor screeched or screamed, Quinne among them. The head pulled out before she could see anything more about it than basic details. It had greenish-gray skin and a beak-like face, along with huge black eyes the size of... well, Quinne didn't want to say dinner plates, since that was such a cliché. The next thing that popped into her head as being comparable were some of her largest dildos. So, sure, its huge black eyes were as wide and Quinne's biggest dildo was long.

All of this passed through Quinne's head in less than the second it took for the head to disappear and the corridor to go quiet again. After that brief moment of shock, though, the hall filled once again with frantic jabber.

"Holyshitholyshitholyshitholy…"

"What the fuck was that!?"

"Mooooooooooommmmmmmm!"

Quinne, even though she was busy babbling herself, instinctively grabbed Amani and slowly pulled her back in the direction they had come.

"Quinne, what was that?" Amani asked. "That looked like a…"

"A sea serpent. Yeah, I know."

"Actually, I was going to say dinosaur."

"Sure, that too. One of those dinosaur sea serpents."

The boy's voice rose from down the hall against the din. "It was a plesiosaurus, Mom! A real live plesiosaurus!"

"A plesiosaurus," Quinne muttered to herself. "Sure, why the hell not?"

"Do you think that was the thing we saw with the whales?" Amani asked. "If it was…"

She didn't finish. The head punched through the wall just a few feet further down from where it had first appeared, although this time with enough force to completely rip away that entire section of wall. There was enough of an opening in the wall now that it could get part of its neck in as well, allowing it to look back and forth down the two different directions. There was no doubt about it now: this was definitely some sort of prehistoric creature, something that should not have existed in the modern world. Beyond that, Quinne's scientific knowledge was completely lacking.

For a moment it looked almost peaceful. The creature cocked its head in a gesture that Quinne would have called curiosity, if the movement hadn't immediately followed such violence. In the space of those few seconds, she could nearly believe that it wasn't going to eat them at all.

Then the head turned away from Quinne and Amani, in the direction of the boy, his nearly nude mother, and whoever her lover might have been. Faster than anyone could follow, the thing's enormous jaws snapped at them. There was a splash and spray of red, leaving the woman and man now wearing a thin sheen of blood along with their sheets and underwear. It took Quinne a second to understand that the two protrusions suddenly growing out from between the monsters teeth were legs.

"No! No! No!" the mother screamed. "You can't…"

On some level she had to know that the plesiosaur wouldn't have any reason to listen, but the plea sounded so genuine, like she thought that maybe, just maybe, the monster would show mercy, open its mouth, and let her son live. Instead the head pulled back again, vanishing outside, leaving everyone in the hall shell-shocked after the unexpected carnage.

"Run," Quinne said to Amani. She was surprised at how

calmly the word came out of her mouth.

"But…" Amani's objection didn't seem to consist of anything more than that one word. If she had anything more coherent to say, the rest of the phrase wouldn't come out.

"Run!" Quinne said, much louder now, and the noise broke her paralysis. She grabbed Amani by the hand, turned, and bolted back in the direction they had come.

There were more sounds behind them: a feminine human scream, the nails-on-chalkboard screech of twisting metal, the shattering of wood or whatever other material had been used to make the decorative interior of the ship, some kind of cut-off gulp from the man, more glass breaking, so many other sounds that Quinne could never hope to identify. Nor did she want to. All of her instincts told her right now that the only thing she truly needed to concentrate on was running, getting as far away from here as possible, and if she could manage it, keeping the sweet young woman beside her safe as well. She was sure that, if her survival needs required it, she would let Amani go in order to save herself, but until such a thing was truly needed she would protect the girl as much as possible. For some reason, the fact that she had been about to sleep with the girl made Quinne feel responsible for her. There wasn't a lot of sense to the desire, but there it was.

Quinne heard the woman's scream for several seconds before it stopped, although she had no way of knowing if it was because the woman had stopped, or if she had run off somewhere to hide, or if she had suffered the same fate as her son. She wanted to look back to see for certain, but the more animalistic part of her brain told her that she couldn't do that, that to look back was equal to death. Instead she concentrated purely on the sounds behind her, her only warning about whether or not the creature was ready to come for the two of them next, as well as the stretch of hall in front of her. The corner they had turned to get here was at least fifty feet ahead, an easy enough distance to cover under normal circumstances. In this instant, however, that space felt infinite, an impossible distance that she would never be able to get across. She couldn't even be sure that they would be safe once they turned that corner and headed back toward the shops and main thoroughfares of the ship. It was simply a short-term goal, an easy to comprehend destination among so many other things that her mind simply couldn't deal with at this time.

Behind her something hit the wall hard enough that she felt the concussion in the air. Then there was another, and she risked looking back just long enough to see the wall immediately behind her bulge from the blow, sending another shower of glass shards against her back along with a spray of near-freezing seawater. Whatever this thing was, it could apparently see her through the windows. She just hoped it wasn't smart enough to see the direction she was going and…

The entire next moment took no more time than a few beats of her rapidly pounding heart. Not even fifteen feet down the hall, she saw the wall begin to bulge. With it she felt and heard the deep bass thud of the plesiosaurus's head hitting the weakened hull. The glass shattered, but there was no time for either Quinne or Amani to raise their arms to shield their eyes. The wall collapsed inward, spraying debris and even more water. The head rammed through, its mouth opening to reveal teeth like a hacksaw and blood-red gullet. No, she only partially realized as she tried to pull back from the attack. Its gullet wasn't actually colored red by itself. That was in fact the blood of the little boy, and possibly his mother and father. She even thought she saw broken bones and ripped flesh deep within the maw, although that might just be some nightmare detail her mind would add to the horrible memory later.

What she was sure of, though, was that they were running too fast. Quinne and Amani were heading right for its mouth.

Quinne put both her feet down, trying to stop their momentum. For a moment she almost lost her footing. She was trying to get it back when the instinctual part of her brain piped up and said "No, lose your footing!" There was no time to give it any rational thought, and if she had that probably would have been the moment she died. Instead she let her balance go, her feet sliding out forward in front of her as they skied over the seawater. Quinne held tight to Amani, pulling her down with her, and it was only halfway through the slide that Quinne realized there was a small gap between the bottom of the monster's jaw and the floor. It was just small enough that any normal sized man probably wouldn't have been able to make it, but both her and Amani were on the petite side. It would be just enough room for them to get through, if, that was, they had enough momentum to slide through the growing puddle of water underneath and come out the other side with enough distance that the creature wouldn't realize what was happening and snap them up at the last second.

Quinne couldn't help herself. She had to close her eyes.

Her senses were reduced to touch, sound, and smell. The water sloshed all around the two of them as, even with her eyes shut, enough light got through her eyelids that she could see the shadow of the monster's head over them. The scent of the water was sharp and briny, but nowhere near as strong as the horrible rotten-fish and coppery-blood stench of the plesiosaurus's breath. Something briefly scraped her nose, like the flesh of something scaly and clammy. They were even close enough that Quinne could hear a gurgle in the creature's throat, like it was trying to find some way to express its dismay that its prey had suddenly disappeared.

Then they were out the other side. Quinne wasted no time yanking Amani further away and to her feet, a feat made difficult but not impossible by the puddles on the polished floor. Quinne thought she could feel the movement of air as the monster tried to twist its head in their new direction, but she didn't dare turn to be sure.

Stumbling to their feet, Quinne and Amani ran down the rest of the length of hall and around the corner. Even when Quinne felt like they were probably a safe distance, she wouldn't let Amani stop.

# CHAPTER FIVE

When they did stop running, it was only because they literally ran into the couple that had been trying to get into the room down the hall. In that minute or two of chaos—*Jesus Christ, was it really only that much time?*—she had completely lost track of anyone else in the hallway other than Amani. Now that they were out of immediate danger, Quinne could spare a thought for the others that might have been caught in the carnage.

The couple had stopped right at the staircase before the hallway came out into the main concourse. They were a young couple dressed in their evening best, and judging from the big rock next to the wedding ring on the woman's finger, Quinne guessed they were likely newlyweds on their honeymoon. Well, it had already proven to be a honeymoon neither of them would forget.

Quinne and Amani turned a corner and hit the woman, who was doubled over with her hands on her knees, trying to catch her breath as her husband leaned against the wall. The woman yelled and almost fell over, but her husband caught her before she hit the floor. Quinne almost expected him to angrily berate them to watch where they were going, then remembered, *Oh yeah, sea monster attack*, and figured the time for politely watching what they were doing was over.

"Okay, I just want to be clear on something," the man said as both Quinne and Amani joined the woman in gasping for breath, although hers had an extra wheeze that sounded like she might have other problems as well. "What I think just happened actually happened, right?"

"Depends on what you think happened," Quinne responded.

"I think a fucking dinosaur just broke into the ship and ate some people."

"Then yeah, that's my understanding as well." She looked back and held her hand up for quiet. The other three obliged, allowing Quinne to listen for sounds of any other attack or people trying to escape. Everything in that direction was silent except for the ever-present hum of the ship's engines.

"Did... did anyone else see if anyone from that family back there escaped?" Amani asked.

It was the woman that responded. "That naked chick was finally running when I last looked back, but I don't know what might have happened after that."

"And the guy she was with?"

"I saw him," the man said in a whisper. "He didn't... you know."

Quinne knew. She also knew that no one needed to ask about the boy. Not a single person in that corridor had missed what happened to him.

"Isn't there supposed to be an alarm or something?" the woman asked.

"I think so," Quinne said, "but maybe nobody knows yet."

"If something huge rips several holes in the side of the ship, I think it would be hard for the captain to not know that something had happened."

"We need to go tell somebody," Amani said. "So they can do a rescue or something like that."

"Rescue?" Quinne asked. "Sweetie, I don't think anyone is going to be able to rescue the people that thing ate."

Amani blanched at the word "ate," as though she hadn't allowed herself to think of what had happened in those terms yet, but she didn't back down. "That's not what I mean. What about all those other cabins up and down that hall? Sure, it's dinner time, but what if there were more people in there? All that has to happen is for them to poke their heads out to see what the fuss is…"

Quinne finally understood. "Right. The longer we wait to tell anyone, the more likely it is that someone else gets taken by that thing. Come on."

Quinne and the three others (the man and woman, between pants, introduced themselves as Jimmy and Wanda) ran the rest of the way back to the main rotunda where they had last seen the captain, but by the time they had reached it, someone had already blown the ship's horns to signal a general emergency. The few safety briefings the passengers had heard during the first days of the cruise told Quinne that this particular sequence of toots typically signaled a fire. She supposed no one had ever bothered to come up with a signal for a sea monster attack, even if the captain finally believed that something was out there.

The main hall was abuzz with activity, including a number of passengers frantically running around looking for children, friends, and loved ones. A team of security people had formed up and were listening to their walkie-talkies, presumably as the captain gave them instructions as to what to do next. Given the lack of utter, incomprehensible terror on the faces of any of the crew, Quinne suspected they still didn't have the all the facts about what had happened.

Neither, apparently, did Quinne and her erstwhile squad. The farther they got into the room, the more she overheard stories and rumors of other things that had happened. There were reports from other places along the same side of the ship of something huge slamming into it. A couple of people who had been on the deck said they thought they'd seen something huge in the water, and the walkie-talkies squawked with news from other members of the crew of holes appearing on the ship. As far as Quinne could tell, though, they were the only ones who had actually seen the creature in action. Or, at least, they were the only ones who had lived long enough to tell about it.

"Hey!" Quinne said, waving her hands in the direction of the security chief. A tag on his uniform identified him as M. Lundgren. "Hey, someone has to get back to my hall. There's a…"

"Ma'am, I need you to stay calm and go back to your room."

"No, listen, we can't go back to our rooms, because…"

"Ma'am, if you don't go back to your room I'll be forced to taser you."

"Wait, what? You don't understand…"

Someone came up to her from behind and shoved her aside as if she were just some debris that had gotten in their way. It took Quinne a moment to remember the guy they had seen earlier. Masterson, she thought.

"There's a sea monster attacking the ship," he said.

"Masterson," Lundgren said. His tone of voice gave Quinne the distinct impression that he'd talked to Masterson before, and he wasn't happy to have to do it ever again. "I should have known you had something to do with this."

"Damn it, man!" Masterson pointed at Lundgren in an overly dramatic gesture that was somehow peculiarly close to a flex. Quinne even though she could see the man's shirt tightening, fighting not to tear. "This has nothing to do with our history and you know it! Every single person on this ship is in danger unless you and your men do something!"

Quinne was pretty sure she could hear an exclamation point at the end of every single one of Masterson's sentences. If this were a comic book, his speech bubbles would have been spiky, excited explosions rather than simple, round bubbles. If he continued speaking at all, he was likely to blow out his vocal cords. She tried to interject.

"Hey, he's right. Down by my room we…"

Lundgren and Masterson continued on as though Quinne

wasn't there. "I'll never forgive you for what you did, Masterson. He was just a puppy. A puppy, for Christ's sakes!"

"Um, hello? Over here?" Quinne asked. "Kind of got really important information about…"

"I did everything I could save him!" Masterson said.

"Okay, this is starting to get ridiculous," Quinne said. "What am I, just some extra in the background here?"

Neither of the men answered her. They just continued to yell at each other over what Masterson had or hadn't done to save Lundgren's Chihuahua fifteen years ago. Quinne tried to keep up for a while, then gave up and turned back to the others.

"Look, the security people are professionals, right? They and the rest of the crew are trained for emergencies like this."

"Emergencies like this?" Wanda asked with a raised eyebrow.

"Okay, maybe not like this. But emergencies in general. And they have to know about the damage. They'll send someone down that way to look for anyone still hiding."

"We can't just let them go over there without knowing what they might run into," Amani said.

"It sounds like Muscles McGee over there knows what really happened just as well as we do, and he's not having much luck convincing Security Chief Lundgren," Quinne said. "And he's a scientist. If Lundgren won't listen to someone like that, he sure as hell won't believe a porn star."

Both Wanda and Jimmy looked surprised, and maybe even a little turned on.

"That buff guy's a scientist?" Wanda asked.

"You're a porn star?" Jimmy asked at the same time.

They both looked at each other with a strange combination of sheepishness and bemusement, as if they both had caught the other thinking something they shouldn't.

"Focus, please. The point I'm trying to make is that we need to find somewhere we'll be safe until someone with far more smarts or power than any of us figures out what to do."

"We're on a boat full of holes," Jimmy said. "I don't really think there's going to be any place safe."

"Oh crap, are we going to sink?" Wanda asked.

Quinne shrugged. "Uh, I don't think so. At least, I hope not? None of the holes in our hall were below the waterline. As long as they stay that way, the ship should be able to continue on just fine."

"And what happens if that thing decides to Swiss cheese some part of the ship that's under the ocean?" Wanda asked.

"Then we'll just have to..." She trailed off as something occurred to her, and from the horrified look the others gave she guessed they'd figured it out, too. Quinne had been about to say that they would just have to get in the lifeboats. The problem was that, in this case, all they would be doing was making it easier for the plesiosaurus, or whatever the hell it was, to turn them all into snacks.

"I'm sure there's a plan," Quinne said. "The captain is probably signaling our distress right now. There will be some kind of rescue coming."

"But what about..." Jimmy started to say, but he was cut off as a man cursed at them from across the room, loud enough that Quinne could clearly hear the creative combination of body parts he strung together even through the confused din of running passengers.

"The hell?" Quinne asked, turning in the man's direction. He was older, either in his late fifties or early sixties, and dressed in a flannel shirt and red trucker's hat. There were a number of other men, as well as a few women, in similar salt-of-the-earth attire, that surrounded him. Despite their age, none of them seemed especially frail, the kind of people who would proudly and belligerently respond, when asked what they did with their lives, that they "worked for a living, goddammit," before turning their heads to spit.

"Her!" the man yelled, pointing in Quinne's direction. "It's got to be her fault!"

"What, me? What the hell did I do?" Quinne asked. Then, upon taking a closer look at the accusing finger, she realized he wasn't pointing at her at all, but rather at Amani standing next to her.

"Oh fudge," Amani muttered.

"Um, am I missing something?" Jimmy asked.

"I've run into these people a couple of times already on the ship," Amani said. "It wasn't pleasant."

"What, is this some kind of farmer's convention?" Wanda asked.

"I don't know, but they were the ones thinking I looked suspicious."

"Oh, for fuck's sake," Quinne said. "There is really not time for petty bigotry." The group of pissed-off looking rednecks started stalking toward them, and although Quinne wanted nothing more than to go up to them and give them a nice verbal lashing of her tongue, she had a feeling that any attempt at confrontation would get ugly quick.

She looked back in the direction of Masterson just in time to see him getting ready to storm off in a huff. And that was really what it looked like he was doing. He had already turned away from Lundgren and was taking deep breaths like he needed to be in the right mindset to stalk off angrily. Realizing she probably didn't have much time to try convincing the burly man to help them, Quinne quickly ran over to him and stood in his way.

"Hey, look, we saw everything, so if you just help us out here..."

Masterson had started moving forward before he realized something was blocking his way. Before Quinne could say anything more, he grabbed her by her upper arms, picked up her scrawny form, set her off to the side, and then walked on as though she had never been there.

"Okay, seriously, are you fucking kidding me?" she yelled after him. He gave no indication that he heard her.

When she turned back to see if the others had seen this, they were gone.

# CHAPTER SIX

For several long moments Quinne had no idea what to do. The chaos and panic seemed to be increasing all around her, and Amani and the newlyweds had disappeared into it, likely to get away from the mob of rednecks who seemed hell-bent on declaring that any brown-skinned woman in a head scarf must be a terrorist. Quinne supposed she had no real reason to try finding them. She'd only met Wanda and Jimmy a few minutes ago, and she had fully expected to never see Amani again after tonight anyway. There was no logical reason for her to be flustered that she couldn't find them. Quinne had come onto the ship alone, she had planned on leaving alone, and apparently now she was going to deal with this crisis alone. She was good at alone. It had served her well so far in her relatively short life.

And yet…

The sheer terror and horror of what was going on here finally started to sink deep into her nerves. She'd been running on adrenaline for the last few minutes, pure survival mode, so it had yet to set in how deep in shit every single person was on this ship. Almost everyone running around knew that something bad was happening, most of them probably realizing they were in deep danger, yet almost none of them understood the nature of it. Yet Quinne had seen it. A dinosaur. A plesiosaurus. An honest-to-God sea monster. She had watched it attack. She had watched it… oh God… oh dear fuck… that little boy…

Quinne dropped to her knees and puked, but no matter how

much her body rejected its contents, she could still smell that stench that came out of the thing's mouth. The rot. The death. The blood. And the noises! She kept hearing them, over and over, the screams, the desperate shouts of the mother, squishing and crunching sounds that she wasn't even sure if she remembered or was just imagining.

Her stomach heaved several more times, but everything she had eaten today had already come out during the first purge. Even with the bile stinging her nostrils, she couldn't get the stench of the creature out of her nose. Looking up, she saw that barely anyone paid any attention to the skinny chick on her knees, ejecting her last shrimp cocktail. Only a few of them even seemed to smell the puddle, and they gave her a wide berth. They had much worse things to worry about, even if they weren't sure what those things were supposed to be.

It occurred to her, as she sat there with her own vomit soaking into the material of her pants, that there was no way she would last very long on her own. It didn't matter how self-sufficient she was, or how smart and resourceful. No one, no matter who they thought they were, would be able to last long in this situation alone. She had to find Amani again, if not for the young woman's sake then at least for her own.

Besides, she still thought Amani was cute.

Quinne painstakingly got back to her feet, managing to avoid slipping back into her own puddle more than once, and then did her best to take a deep breath and try to figure out the chaos around her. Looking around, she realized that there were security cameras high up in every corner. No matter what Lundgren had said to Masterson, someone in charge must have seen what had happened in that hallway, or at the very least would see what had happened once they reviewed the security footage. The footage would do a far better job of convincing people than Quinne could. Informing people did not have to be her first priority. She could instead concentrate on finding her group.

She went back to exactly where she had last seen Amani and the newlyweds, although it wasn't like she expected there to be some big clue she could follow. She tried to ask a few people in the area if they had seen anything, but they tended to have more questions for her regarding what was happening, and Quinne wasn't sure how much she could say without sounding completely off her rocker. She wandered out onto the deck by the swimming pool, getting distracted yet again the fact that the pool even existed. Seriously, if the Letroix Corporation had known in advance that this ship would be used primarily for their arctic cruises, then how stupid did the people in charge have to be to think it needed an outdoor pool? She'd only see one brave soul try to swim in it on her second day. Despite the fact that it was supposedly heated, the guy had come out looking like an icicle.

But the expanse of the pool also provided her with a wide open spot across which she could look without people crowding in her way, and after looking around it for nearly a minute she thought she saw the flash of a familiar red trucker's hat on the other side. There weren't as many people to shove through here, allowing Quinne to get around to the other side with plenty of time to see Amani back up against a lounge chair and trip over it, causing her to spill rather close to the pool. Wanda and Jimmy were between her and the group of rednecks, who had shrunk down to only four people now. Quinne wasn't sure what had happened to the rest of them, but the one in the trucker's hat had apparently decided he was the leader of the group.

"Look, I don't have no problem with black people," Trucker's Hat said. "Just get out of the way and let us take that bitch to where security can lock her up."

"How many times do I have to tell you she didn't do anything?" Wanda said.

"Don't be naïve, girl," one of the others in the group, the only woman who had stayed behind to be part of the mob, said with a haughty tilt of her head. "She had to be the one that did it. If she didn't, then why is she on the ship alone?"

"Um, that logic doesn't make any sense," Jimmy said.

"You trying to get cute, boy?" Trucker Hat said. "We know what's smart and what isn't.

"Boy?" Jimmy asked. "Uh-uh, you better rethink pulling that racist shit on me."

"Oh, pulling the race card now?" one of the other men in the group asked. "Well, I'll have you know that it's not even possible for me to be racist. I have black friends!"

Jimmy looked like he wanted to slug the bastard, but he knew damn well how horribly that would go downhill. Quinne knew they could take care of themselves, but she also figured there had to be something she could do to help. "Hey!" Quinne yelled at them. The woman glanced at her briefly, but otherwise she might as well have been nothing more than the scum on the bottom of these people's shoes.

"Fine," she muttered to herself. "Guess it's time to pull out the big guns. Well, little guns, but they're high caliber." She unzipped her coat and then lifted up her shirt. "I said 'Hey,' you bastards!"

This time one of the men looked first before looking away, then did a wide-eyed double take. "Holy Mary Mother of God," he whispered. This caused the rest of them to turn as well, with Trucker Hat looking last. Out of all of them, however, he was the only one who had the sudden look of recognition.

*Looks like I've got a fan here*, Quinne thought.

"Yeah, that's right!" Quinne shouted. "You recognize the girls, don't you?"

The woman turned to glare at Trucker Hat. "Hank, you better not know that skank."

*Hank*, Quinne thought. *Somehow I just knew this guy had to be a Hank. Shitheads like this are always Hank.*

"Uh, no honey. Of course I... oh wow, that fairy tattoo is new, isn't it?"

The tattoo in question was over a year old, which meant that this guy probably knew her best from her early cam-show days. Considering this guy was probably old enough to be her grandfather, the thought gave Quinne a rare moment of squick.

"You cheating bastard!" the woman yelled, shoving Hank into the pool. He didn't even have a chance to surface before she dove in after him, her fingers tensed into talons that she probably intended to use to gouge his pervy old eyes out.

The remaining three rednecks scattered. All the other random bystanders that had been near the pool were also running away, but Quinne didn't pay much attention to that. She pulled down her shirt and ran over to help Amani up.

"Oh holy hell, I think I finally recognize those breasts," Wanda said. "Aren't you Quinne Quiver? My last boyfriend jacked off to you all the time."

"I can sign autographs later," Quinne said. "Right now my nipples are so cold they could cut glass, so I need to get back inside. And probably it's a good idea to do that before Thing One and Thing Two over there remember their irrational hatred of anyone that doesn't glow in the dark."

"Thanks," Amani said to Quinne, holding her hand tight.

"No problem. Happy to help."

"Oh. No, I don't mean for that," Amani said, gesturing at the couple still wrestling in the pool. "I think Jimmy and Wanda had it. I meant thanks for the free show." She grinned in a not entirely innocent way, and Quinne gave her the same smoldering look back.

"Consider yourself lucky. Normally people have to pay a subscription for that view."

"Hey, is there something else going on?" Wanda asked, gesturing out at the edge of the deck. Quinne hadn't been paying attention to where everyone else was going before, but now she saw that the crowds of people had congregated along the railings and were peering down into the water at the base of the ship.

"Uh oh," Quinne said. She waved her arms and shouted at the people as she ran in that direction, not that they were paying any attention to her. She would have tried the shirt trick again, but there were kids among the crowd over here. "Hey, get away from there! You don't want to be..." She stopped when she got close enough to see through the crowd. "Oh wow. And also, fuck me running."

One of the nearby parents turned and gave Quinne a sour look. "Language! This is a family ship!"

"Um, right. Sorry."

"What is it?" Amani asked as she ran up behind Quinne. The crowd was thick enough here that the young woman couldn't quite shove her way to the front.

"We're screwed, that's what," Quinne said.

"Why?" Wanda asked.

"Remember that thing we saw in the hall?" Quinne asked.

"Yeah?"

"It has a friend."

# CHAPTER SEVEN

"What is that?" some little kid to Quinne's right asked his mother.

"I think it's a whale," the mother said, although the tone of her voice told Quinne that she was pretty sure she was incorrect. Quinne was pretty sure as well, but she was damned if she could identify the thing with a proper name. It was certainly as big as a whale, maybe even more so. In fact, Quinne thought the ghastly bloody chunk of flesh it was toying with in its mouth might be the remains of a whale, most likely one of the ones she and Amani had seen slaughtered earlier.

Amani finally shoved her way up next to Quinne. "That's not a whale," she said quietly. "That's a liopleurodon."

"A who-what-now?" Jimmy asked.

"Another prehistoric sea creature," Amani said. "Like the plesiosaurus we saw earlier."

"How do you even know that?" Wanda asked.

"Don't you remember that really old YouTube meme?" Amani asked. "The one with the unicorn?" Her voice switched over to a creepy sing-song. "Charlie. Chaaaarliieee. We're going to Candy Mountain. Caaaandy Moooountain!"

Quinne and the newlyweds stared at her.

"Uh, yeah," Amani said, looking away. "Anyway, there was a liopleurodon in it."

Quinne supposed she had probably seen the thing in the water before in some illustration or other of ancient sea creatures, but it was entirely different to see the thing in the flesh. If she was forced to compare it to some more mundane creature of the world, she would say the liopleurodon resembled an alligator, but that would be like saying a garden snake resembled a giant Amazonian anaconda. Quinne had no way of knowing if this thing's size was typical for the species, but it made the whales they had seen earlier look like puppies. It had gray skin mottled with green, and instead of feet it had four massive flippers, each one big enough to capsize a schooner. It was monstrous, a thing capable of mass destruction.

Which made it all the more incongruous that the thing appeared to be playing.

Quinne cocked her head and watched quizzically as the liopleurodon tossed the chunk of whale meat from its snout and out into the ocean, then sped off in chase of it. Once it had the meat in its mouth once more, it took just enough time to chew off a chunk before repeating the whole process. The giant, prehistoric killing machine actually looked like it was having fun.

The crowd around them murmured nervously, as though no one was sure whether they should be afraid for their lives or else amazed and entertained. For just those few seconds, Quinne fell on the side of entertained. Separated from the earlier events, this was objectively amazing. A dinosaur. There was an actual, honest-to-God dinosaur swimming in the Arctic Ocean directly in front of them. She had no idea how this had happened, but really, the how didn't matter. It just was, and it was amazing.

"Is that what caused the ship to shake?" someone in the crowd asked. A number of people rushed to answer, even though none of them actually *knew* the answer. While Quinne herself knew, she kept quiet. Scanning the water, she couldn't find any sign of the plesiosaurus that actually had attacked the ship, but that had been on the other side of the *Lucky Lady Duck*. She backed away from the railing, gesturing for her three companions to come with her.

"Two dinosaurs," Quinne said when she was out of hearing

range of most of the others. "One dinosaur is unlikely enough, but two?"

"That's some *Jurassic Park* shenanigans going on there," Jimmy said.

"*Jurassic Park* isn't real, honey," Wanda said. Then, quietly to Quinne, "Really, don't get him started. He has a legit fear of velociraptors."

"Doesn't matter whether or not it's real," Jimmy said. "This right here is. And what do you want to bet that if there's two dinosaurs…"

"Then there's a good chance that there's more," Quinne said. "And our little cruise ship just so happened to sail right through their school, or whatever you would call it."

"How long before we come out the other side of this school?" Amani asked.

Quinne shrugged. "I don't know. That probably depends a lot on what the captain and his crew decides."

"Well, at least this one doesn't appear to be that interested in us," Wanda said.

From somewhere down the deck someone shouted, "Everyone, stand aside! I can take care of this!"

"Um, for some reason I get the impression that it's not going to ignore us for much longer," Jimmy said, pointing the direction of the voice. The all turned to see Lundgren and a number of his other security people coming toward them, most of them with weapons drawn. Mostly they carried Tasers, but a few had hand guns. Lundgren himself had a harpoon gun.

"Oh for the love of shit on a bun," Quinne said. "Really?"

"Everyone get out of the way," Lundgren said. He shoved a couple of the passengers, ignoring their indignant cries until he himself was finally at the railing. "Whatever is out there, we'll be the ones who…" He stopped as he saw the liopleurodon frolicking in the waves lapping off the side of the ship. "Oh shit. It's an alligator."

"Actually," Amani started to say, "I'm pretty sure it's…"

"Amani, hon, don't," Quinne said. "Something tells me he wouldn't be able to pronounce liopleurodon even if he tried."

"To be fair, I'm not even sure if any of us can," Wanda said.

"Really, folks, I need you all to step away," Lundgren called out again. Then, when no one showed much interest in doing what he said, he grabbed a handgun from one of his subordinates, pointed it straight up in the air, and fired. Several passengers screamed or jumped, but every single one of them suddenly decided there were much more interesting places to be than at the railing. None of them went any farther than they absolutely had to, though. It was pretty obvious that they were about to get a show far more interesting than watching aging magicians sawing a capybara in half.

Quinne was about to step forward and tell him that she thought that would be a bad idea, but before she could there was more shouting from down the deck, followed by Masterson's two companions Mickey and Gordon running up to join them. They stopped a few feet away from Lundgren, both of them taking a moment to look down at their feet as if there was some specific mark here that they were supposed to be on.

"You have to stop," Gordon said. Quinne could have almost swear that his eyes flicked back and forth as though he were reading cue cards that only he could see. "If you attack that liopleurodon, the situation will only get worse."

"Yeah, like, much worse," Mickey said. "Crazy kooky worse. Rabbit in a blender worse. Peanut butter and avocado sandwiches worse."

Quinne looked at Amani. "You think maybe he thinks he's being funny?"

Amani nodded. "Like the designated comic relief, except written by someone who doesn't actually know how humor works.

I'm kind of surprised at how well combed his hair is."

"Fifteen bucks says that next time we see him, his hair is all mussed up like he's a mad scientist that just got of bed."

"I'm not one for betting," Amani said.

"I'll take that bet," Jimmy said. "What about you, Wanda? Want in on that action?"

"Nuh-uh. That's fifteen dollars you're going to lose, love."

"Look, you crazy numbnuts," Lundgren said to Mickey. "I have no idea what a leahplurpladon is supposed to be, but I do know that I'm responsible for the safety of this ship. I have the absolute authority to do whatever is needed, by the power invested in me by the Letroix Corporation."

"I highly doubt that a company that pays people to dress up as cartoon ducks on their cruise lines has a right to say anything when it comes to the creatures of the ocean," Mickey said.

"Quinne, we should get out of here," Amani said. "I've got a feeling it's not going to be very safe over in this area in just a few minutes."

"I think you're right. And also, if I continue listening to those guys, I think some of my brain cells are going to die."

It was rather easy for the four of them to back out of the crowd, as there were more and more people arriving to see what all the fuss was about and were eager to take the place of Quinne and the others at the railing. It was also easy now to find a place on the deck near the main entrance inside that was relatively calm. Anyone that wasn't trying to see the new arrival in the sea must be inside somewhere, likely in cabins, shops, and restaurants where they thought they would be safe until the *Lucky Lady Duck* either got out of danger or help arrived.

"We need to do something," Amani said.

"There's nothing we *can* do, sweetie," Wanda said.

"But there're sea monsters out there! Actual dinosaurs!"

"Wanda's right, Amani," Quinne said. "We're not action

heroes. If this were a movie, we would be the background characters no one notices. Our whole purpose would be to run around screaming so the real action stars would look all the more stoic."

"Right," Jimmy said. "Except I don't see any of the four of us running around with our hands in the air doing Kermit flails, do you?"

"I guess not," Quinne said. "That still doesn't tell us what we should be doing."

"Maybe we should go back in the direction of your rooms," Amani said. "The crew has to be doing something there, trying to fix the holes or something."

"Sure, if they didn't get snatched," Wanda said.

"No, we would have noticed if there were any more attacks," Quinne said. "The whole fucking ship shook, remember? Maybe you're right. Maybe they need volunteers."

"Uh-uh. I'm not going back there," Jimmy said. "Not until we're safely docked somewhere that's not crawling with sea serpents."

"Maybe we can find that Masterson guy, then," Quinne said. "Even if he is an ass, he looked like he might have had a plan."

Several gunshots rang out from the crowd at the railing. They all jerked their heads in that direction as they heard Mickey and Gordon yelling something incoherent at Lundgren.

"Or we could just wait for the idiot security guard to do something to start up the action again," Quinne said.

They all stood completely still, waiting for the liopleurodon to give some roar or for the entire ship to shake with an attack. After several seconds Jimmy said, "Maybe he missed."

"Or maybe that thing's so huge that it wouldn't even notice a couple of gunshots," Wanda said.

"Or maybe we should just wait for it," Amani said.

"Wait for what?" Jimmy asked.

"She's right," Quinne said. "Wait for it. Waaaaait for it…"

One second of nothing. Two seconds. Three.

And then there was the explosion.

"Called it," Quinne and Amani said at the same time. It would have been cute if the entire ship didn't erupt once again into chaos.

# CHAPTER EIGHT

While the crowd at the railing scattered, Quinne scanned all around them for some sign of what exactly had happened. The horn blew again to sound a general emergency, but that did little to explain the situation. Quinne ran back up to Lundgren, the only person still standing at the railing. At least technically. There was one other person, but she wasn't so much standing there as hanging over the side of the railing by one hand. Even though she screamed for help, Lundgren continued to do nothing but stare at her slack-jawed, the handgun in one hand and the now-empty harpoon gun in the other.

"What are you doing?" Quinne yelled at him. "Help her!"

"I don't even think I hit it," Lundgren said. "It just went below the water right after the shot. I don't know what I did…"

"Idiot!" Quinne reached and grabbed the woman's arm with both hands, but the woman was slick with sea spray and Quinne's hands had gone sweaty. Quinne looked down into her eyes, and every detail of the woman's face etched itself in her mind. She looked to be in her mid to late forties, with shoulder-length curly black hair and a complexion that clearly showed she had come out the other side of a bad patch of acne when she was younger. Her clothes were modest, middle to lower class. Quinne caught the glint of a wedding ring on the hand that wasn't holding the railing, also modest, the kind that said she and her husband didn't need to prove anything to the world. *Where is he right now?* Quinne wondered. *Why isn't he the one trying to hold her back from plunging into the deep*? So many different possible answers, none of which she could get with what meager information she currently had. Quinne did see a Star of David hanging from a simple chain that dangled just outside the woman's coat, and down the woman's neckline Quinne could see what might have been a small tattoo on her chest, although she couldn't make out any details.

All these things she would always remember, but none so much as the look of absolute, unbridled terror in the woman's eyes. This woman had a pretty good idea what was about to happen, and she was clearly not ready for it.

"Please," the woman said. "Bobby…"

Quinne never did find out who Bobby was. He could have been her husband, her son, her lover—hell, he could have been the janitor at her elementary school for all Quinne knew. Because whatever message she wanted Quinne to deliver to this Bobby, it was drowned out by the enormous splash of sea water when the liopleurodon leaped up from the ocean, heading straight up for the woman dangling like bait from above.

Quinne let go and backed away.

The woman's grip slipped from the railing, and she was already falling into the monster's gullet long before it reached the apex of its jump. The creature's jaw slammed shut as it continued to rise, then did a backwards flop like a whale breaching. The splash it made was enough to douse the deck and drench Quinne, and it was possible she might have slipped and fallen overboard herself if she hadn't already put a few feet of distance between her and the railing. As the water rained down and subsided, and the liopleurodon vanished back into the deep blue, Quinne stood in place, absolutely motionless, barely even breathing.

"Quinne!" Amani yelled from behind her. A few seconds later she felt the young woman's hand on her shoulder, but Quinne didn't react. She couldn't react. All she could continue doing was staring out over the railing. Her eyes refused to move, even blink, as though if she did anything at all she would have to start coming to grips with what she had just done.

And with thought, the dam holding back the flood of her thoughts broke. *I let go. I had her and I let go. I could have saved her. If Lundgren had helped I would have been able to pull her up. Even when he didn't, I still could have done something. I let go. I could have swung her to the side, out of its way. Something. Anything. I let her go. I'm alive. It didn't get me. Twice in one day I almost died. I let her go. I'm alive. It's a monster. I'm a monster. I let her go. I let her go. I let her go.*

"Quinne? Quinne! Can you hear me?"

"Oh shit, what's wrong with her?"

"Quinne?" A couple of finger snaps in front of her face. "Quinne, snap out of it. There's no time for this."

"She's BSOD."

"She's what?"

"Blue screen of death. Like on a computer that's crashed?"

"Quinne, listen to me, there's nothing you could have done. You already did more than anyone else could have been expected to. If Lundgren had helped…"

"Wait, where the hell did he go, anyway?"

"I don't know, somewhere in that direction? Piece of shit ran as soon as Quinne had her."

"If only I had been faster, I could have helped."

"I let her go," Quinne whispered, her words barely audible even to herself.

"What? What was that you said?"

"Look, we've got to get her away from the edge of the deck. Something else is going on. Look over that way, don't you see?"

"Oh fudge. What even is that?"

"Smoke, but don't ask me from what. Let's at least get her over into that doorway."

Quinne blinked, suddenly realizing that her eyes had begun to sting from the salt water and keeping them open. She blinked again, such a simple motion, but in that moment it felt full of power, something she willed herself to do. First her eyelids, then she moved her feet, shuffling at first before taking real steps. She became vaguely aware of three sets of hands guiding her, moving her somewhere safe. Just like that time in the park when she had been a teenager, the people that had found her and taken her to the hospital. Just like after…

She wouldn't think on that, and with that her brain started working properly again, like it had needed the threat of the horrible memory coming back to her as a way to reboot her mind. Slowly, awareness of her environment returned. She was on a ship. She was surrounded by friends. Okay, maybe not real friends, considering she had only just met all three of them, but they would do what they could to keep her safe. She was safe, at least for the moment. She was safe.

*I let her go.*

Yes, she had. She had saved herself when she could have tried saving someone else as well. But that was something she would have to deal with later. Let it haunt her at whatever future date. For now, in this moment, if she wanted to continue surviving, she needed her mind, body, and soul to get back in full working order.

"Quinne? Are going to be okay?" Amani. She stood directly in front of Quinne, her hands on Quinne's shoulders, holding her steady. The girl Quinne had been about to sleep with. It wouldn't have been anything more than a pleasant night followed by the two of them going their separate ways. Except now, with Amani looking into her eyes and making sure that Quinne was still all there, Quinne felt a much deeper connection quicken. This wasn't a bond that could be formed by simple sex. This was a deep understanding of what it meant to walk through Hell.

"No," Quinne finally managed. "At least not later. For now though, I guess I can function."

"Good," Amani said, clearly relieved. "Good."

"I didn't catch everything you guys said, but did someone mention smoke?"

"Near the back of the ship," Wanda said. "I'm thinking it's probably where the explosion came from."

Wanda and Jimmy took point leading the group out of their cozy little doorway hidey-hole and to a place where they could all see the column of greasy black smoke rising up from the back of the ship. As they crossed the deck they encountered pockets of chaos. A father stumbled back and forth, calling out names through a haze of tears. If Quinne had to guess, she'd say they were his wife and children. A sudden stab of panic and horror went through Quinne's chest as she wondered if this might be the doomed woman's Bobby. That sickening sensation lessened only a little when a woman ran up to him and gave him a hug, before the two of them both went off together, desperately calling out the names of their children.

A young man in his early twenties came out a door, screaming hysterically that the theater area was swarming with giant killer rats. It took Quinne a few seconds to realize the infamous capybaras had probably gotten loose. The most surreal sight of all, though, was Lucky Lady Duck herself, in all her oversized fuzzy cartoon costume glory, wandering dazedly around with blood streaming down the front of her suit. Amani wanted to stop and help, or at the very least make sense of what was going on, but the performer in the Lucky Lady Duck costume finally collapsed in a chair and removed her oversized waterfowl head, revealing a frazzled blond woman underneath with blood seeping from her scalp. Whatever had happened to her, it had to have been bad if it caused that kind of wound even through the cushioning of the giant plush head.

"Anyone know anything about medicine?" Quinne said quietly, nodding her head in the direction of the woman. She looked like she was about to pass out.

"I'm a nurse," Jimmy said. "Wanda, can you help me?" The two of them jogged off in the direction of the young woman. Quinne wanted to follow and help, but the face of the woman dangling over the water floated back into her mind, and Quinne stopped herself. She couldn't help. She would get in the way. All that would happen if she jumped in was that someone else would get hurt. Amani, whether she realized what was going through Quinne's head or not, at least appeared to see that Quinne needed to be distracted. "Look," Amani said, pointing at the smoke. "Any idea where that's coming from?"

"Back of the ship somewhere? Engines, maybe? I honestly don't know enough about the design of cruise ships to say. And even if I did, that probably wouldn't do me any good on this one."

"But what would have caused it?"

"Well, I'm sure those rednecks that got stuck playing in the pool are going to try to say you set a bomb."

"Please tell me you don't really believe that."

"Of course I don't really believe that. Even if you haven't been with me this entire time, I'm not some bigot who automatically assumes anyone wearing a headscarf must be a radical terrorist. Plus, also, you know. There's the whole sea monster thing. Logic says this has something to do with that."

"You think the plesiosaurus did something?"

Quinne shrugged. "I'm as clueless as every other damned tourist in the background here. Maybe if we really want answers, we should try to find Gordon, Mickey, and Masterson again."

"You really think they know anything?"

"Not in the slightest. But they obviously think they know things, which is at least a step up from where we are. Maybe we should try to find them."

"And where exactly would we do that?"

Quinne gestured at the black column. "Where there's smoke."

# CHAPTER NINE

Amani and Quinne briefly debated whether to go right away or wait for Jimmy and Wanda, but the argument became moot when the newlyweds slowly walked up to join them. Quinne could already guess what had happened based on the dejected way Jimmy walked and the gentle way Wanda held his hand, but she looked back in the direction they had come anyway. The young woman lay completely motionless in the chair, her head lolled to the side and her eyes closed. She made an odd tableau, with the peaceful expression on her mouth, her bloody head and face, and the oversized duck suit making her head tiny. A combination of somber, violent, and ridiculous, all in one scene. "She'd already stopped breathing by the time I got to her," Jimmy said. "I didn't have any equipment to help, and I couldn't figure out how to get the stupid suit off to try to revive her."

"I don't suppose anyone knew her name?" Quinne asked.

Wanda shrugged. "Lucky Lady Duck? You know how the Letroix Corporation is regarding the actors they have playing their characters. They do absolutely nothing to dispel the illusion for the kids and families."

Quinne looked away from the girl's body. "I'm sure that anyone who comes across her now is going to have their illusion dispelled pretty fucking handily."

"You think we should move her?" Amani asked. "So that, I don't know, some kid doesn't find her and get traumatized?"

"I'm pretty sure that any kids on the ship are going to see

plenty more to traumatize them before the day is out," Quinne said. "Still…" Quinne looked around her and found a coat that had been discarded on the deck at some point during the running and screaming. She picked it up and gently placed it over Lucky Lady Duck's real face. For a few seconds she stared down at the corpse before saying, "I'm going to call her Sarah. Just until we maybe find out what her real name was. Unless anyone else has something they think is more fitting?"

"Nah," Jimmy said quietly. "Sarah seems like a nice enough name."

They made their way toward the back of the ship with an odd mixture of hurry and leisure. Hurry because they all felt a clear sense that, whatever had happened, it wasn't over. Leisure because, well, if it wasn't over, then they didn't want to be right on top of the next part of this disaster, did they? Yet they had no idea where else they were supposed to go. It was a sense of confused desperation Quinne saw in almost everyone they passed. Everyone knew the disaster wasn't over, but they didn't know when it would start up again or even what it was. Quinne kept expecting she would hear another series of horns in warning or an announcement over the ship-wide intercom telling everyone what kind of emergency this was, what they should do, where they should go. Yet there was nothing.

Apparently Quinne wasn't the only one thinking along those lines. "Why isn't the captain doing or saying anything?" Amani asked.

"Maybe something happened to him," Wanda said.

"Even if something did, there's still protocol," Jimmy said. "He's got to have a second and third and fourth in command. If he weren't able to do the job, there should be others to step up."

"Maybe we're in the midst of one of those really colossal screw ups you see on the news," Quinne said. "Like that cruise ship that just up and tipped over, and the captain abandoned ship like a little bitch."

"There's hundreds, maybe thousands of people on this ship," Wanda said. "Hundreds of people going through shit, and right along with them hundreds of reasons the captain isn't taking charge the way he should. None of us will probably find out until we're off the ship and watching all the coverage on the news."

"Sure, if we get off the ship," Jimmy said.

"I think I heard something earlier from one of the crew about calling for a rescue," Amani said. "There's got to be someone or something on the way."

"Either that or the ship will get out of the range of those things," Wanda said. "They wouldn't follow us all the way back to civilization, would they?"

"Too many questions, and we're not going to get any answers," Quinne said.

Jimmy stopped to check on a group of teenagers that had found a spot to huddle just inside one of the doors. One of them was bleeding from the arm, and it took some cajoling to let him look at the wound. While Wanda tried to chat the teens up to get them to relax, Amani cocked her head at Quinne. "Do you think that whatever's going on here has anything to do with that thing that happened down in Mexico a couple months ago?"

At first Quinne didn't understand what she was asking, but then there weren't many major news events that happened in Mexico that could be compared to mysterious happenings in the Arctic. "You mean that shit that happened off the Baja Peninsula?"

"I guess. All I remember is that it happened down in Mexico and the video was all over Facebook for a while."

"Yeah, I remember. People stopped talking about it when that gorilla got shot," Quinne said. "I don't know, though. I always kind of figured that had to be fake. I mean, the girl who supposedly beat that giant-ass shark got her own reality show or something, right?"

"I also heard she lost her leg. Kind of hard to fake that. And given that we've so far been attacked by both a plesiosaurus and a liopleurodon, is a giant hammerhead shark really that far-fetched?"

"I guess not. Man, when we get out of this, we can totally sign book deals or something. *If* we get out of this."

They both stopped talking for several seconds as Quinne's words registered with them both. Quinne thought of Sarah, and the woman over the railing (Becky, Quinne decided, just so the woman wouldn't be nameless forevermore), and then wondered about them. If she and Amani died here, would anyone see? Would someone determine that they needed a name as they remembered what had happened to them? Or would anyone remember the way they died at all? Would they just be random names on the manifest? Would all of Quinne's subscribers find out what had happened? Or would they just sit and wonder, "Hey, why the hell doesn't Quinne Quiver post videos of herself with a dildo and butt plug anymore?"

Was that really all her life would amount to, to some people? Not that Quinne regretted any of her decisions in life. She'd lived her own damn way, and fuck anyone that had a problem with it. But she felt a strange sadness at the idea that so few people would even know that Quinne Quiver, tattooed kinkster extraordinaire, was the same as Laurie Schnellmann, just another casualty during the doomed final odyssey of the *Lucky Lady Duck*.

"My legal name is Laurie Schnellmann," Quinne told Amani in a hushed voice.

"Huh?"

"Just in case, you know? If anything happens. Really, I consider myself Quinne, not Laurie, but if I die, I just wanted someone to know…"

She couldn't get herself to finish. She didn't have to. Amani responded by taking her hand and squeezing it gently, then bringing it to her lips and kissing it. Nothing sexual about it, just a simple gesture of intimacy. Quinne took Amani's hand and did the same.

Wanda and Jimmy joined them again soon after. The teen really should have had stitches, Jimmy said, but he didn't have anything to sew with and the cut wouldn't be life threatening as long as the teens didn't do anything stupid.

The closer they got to the back of the boat, the more Quinne had a sense that something wasn't right. Although she'd rather not get anywhere near the railing anymore, especially when some giant creature could smack into the ship again at any moment, she still forced herself to look over the side. "Shit," she said. "That's probably not good."

"What?" Amani asked.

"I don't think the ship is moving anymore. At least not under its own power."

All of them looked over the side just long enough to be certain for themselves that she was right, then continued along. The closer they got to the back, the more activity there seemed to be. Nearer the front, any passengers who hadn't found someplace inside to hide had taken on a lethargic, doomed aspect, as though there was absolutely nothing they could do until they were given orders by the captain or some Coast Guard boat showed up to rescue them. Back here, however, there was a very different feel. People rushed about with obvious destinations, and while most of them couldn't exactly be called calm, they at least weren't running to and fro in a panic. The reason for this became apparent as they reached the large aft deck and saw someone standing on some kind of equipment to give everyone a better view of him. Masterson. And nearby, his two buddies were standing as though they were his enforcers.

"Pay up," Quinne said to Jimmy.

"Huh?"

"Mickey's hair. It's mad scientist city. You owe me fifteen

bucks."

"Uh, all my money is back in our rooms."

"Yeah, well, don't worry about it for now. I bet you're good for it."

"Was that supposed to be a pun?"

"Was *what* supposed to be a pun?"

"You said you bet."

"Don't be ridiculous. I'm way too exhausted to do puns on purpose."

Mickey's hair was indeed messed up, and there was soot and dirt all over his face, same as Gordon. Quinne couldn't help but think, though, that there was something theatrical about the way the mess was smeared on them. They looked less like they'd gone through horrible shit and more like they had spent an hour in a Hollywood makeup chair. Masterson looked even better. He only had a single smudge at his temple and a cut on his cheek, perfectly positioned so that it would give him a nice manly scar when it healed.

"Okay, listen up!" Masterson boomed at the gathered people. That was really the only correct word for it, *boomed.* "I've got some bad news! The captain and most of his main people are dead!"

A shudder of horror through the crowd. Quinne glanced at her companions to see looks of pure terror that were probably mirrored on her own face. That explained the lack of further directions.

"We need to not panic, though! Rescue is coming!" Masterson bassed. Again, that was the only word for it, "bassed," a deep and heavy tone that nearly shook the floor beneath them.

"How is he even doing that?" Amani whispered to Quinne.

"Seriously, I honestly think this guy had to be a pro-wrestler in another life," Quinne said. "He talks to groups the way the heroic baby-face would talk to an arena full of people."

"The captain managed to call for help before the monster got him!" Masterson exploded. "There will be rescue helicopters soon! Before we lost contact, they assured me that there would be three large copters on the way, more than enough to rescue everyone here!"

*Wait, what?* Quinne exchanged looks with her companions, checking to see if they found his words as worrisome as she did. She saw very clear discomfort from all three of them. For the first time, Quinne took a clear look at the people that formed the crowd. Although Quinne and the others had come close enough to hear Masterson speak, they were still far enough removed that they couldn't be considered part of the group. Not that they could ever hope to be considered part of this group anyway. They were a heavily tattooed queer millennial, a young woman unapologetic in the garb of her religion, and a young black couple. The crowd, on the other hand, was overwhelmingly light skinned, older, and judging from their clothes, well-to-do. They certainly hadn't gotten onto this ship using coupons and rebates like Quinne had. And to these people, they really might as well have been the only people on the entire ship. The people in the cheaper rooms were barely people at all, and certainly the staff and crew were nothing more to them than props.

It didn't even occur to a single person in this group, Quinne realized as she scanned their faces, that there was anyone worth rescuing other than themselves. Three helicopters would be fine to them.

"Anyone else doing this math?" Quinne quietly asked.

"Sure am," Wanda said.

"Wait a second," a well-dressed white woman in her sixties said from the crowd. For a moment Quinne thought she would be the one to bring up the flaw in the escape plan, but her mind was obviously caught on one earlier detail. "Did you honestly just say that the captain was eaten by a monster?"

"I did! I know it sounds crazy, but I'm a scientist! I know

what I'm talking about!" Masterson exploded.

"Uh, what kind of scientist, exactly?" someone else in the crowd asked.

"Does it matter? I fucking love science, and I'm a scientist!"

Amani said something in a language Quinne didn't know. She assumed Amani was swearing. "You've got to be kidding me."

"What?" Quinne asked.

"All this time everyone's probably been assuming that this guy knew what he was talking about. But it sounds to me like he thinks he gets to call himself a scientist just because he follows a Facebook group."

"Look, I know five surprising facts about the creature that's been attacking the ship!" Masterson ejaculated. "I can keep us all safe until the rescue choppers get here!"

"Oh, you have got to be kidding me," Quinne muttered.

"What would you call that thing he's doing with his voice right now, anyway?" Wanda asked.

"Ejaculating. He definitely ejaculated that sentence."

"I don't think that word means what you think it means," Jimmy said.

Quinne shrugged. "Trust me. I definitely know all the meanings of that word. It's the only way I can describe it. He's talking in the kind of speech tags that you would find in the pulp novel of a really garbage writer."

"If everyone here just remains patient," Masterson rumbled, "and does everything I say, then I promise you that you will be safe soon!"

Quinne couldn't hold herself back anymore. She ran up to the edge of the crowd and yelled at Masterson. "Three helicopters isn't going to be enough! There's got to be almost a thousand people on this ship!"

Several people turned to stare at her. All it took was one look at the hints of tattoos poking out near her neck and hands for them to decide she wasn't someone they needed to pay attention to. Masterson didn't even give her that much. He stepped down from his perch as though no one had even spoken, then leaned over to whisper in Gordon's ear for a few seconds before announcing that he had important things to do before the choppers got here.

As the crowd broke into several nervously milling groups, Gordon made his way through the crowd to Quinne. "Young lady, did you need some help?" Gordon asked.

"No, I don't need some help. I need to know how the hell three helicopters are going to be enough to save every single person on this cruise ship."

"You don't need to worry," Gordon said, putting a hand on her shoulder. She shimmied out of his grip. Gordon looked at her as though that were the rudest thing he'd ever witnessed.

"You don't get to tell me what I can and cannot worry about when we're in the middle of the Arctic Ocean being attacked by sea monsters. Is there a real plan, or not?"

"The helicopters will have to go back and forth to safety, okay? I'm former U.S. Coast Guard. I know how this works."

Quinne had a suspicion that this guy knew about as much about the Coast Guard as Masterson knew about science, especially considering they weren't anywhere near United States waters.

"So, what, these people get rescued," she gestured at the well-to-do passengers getting increasingly agitated around her as she spoke, "while the rest of us just sit around waiting? The ship is damaged, isn't it? It could be sinking, for all we know. By the time the choppers get back for a second load, we could all be gone."

"Everyone will be fine," Gordon said. "The ship isn't sinking. There's just a few mechanical problems after the last attack by the creature."

"A few mechanical problems?" Quinne asked. She gestured at the plume of smoke still coming out from the very back of the ship. It wasn't as thick as it had been earlier, but it certainly didn't look like it was stopping yet. "You're seriously going to try telling me that this isn't anything to worry about?"

"Miss, please," Gordon said. "You're upsetting the passengers."

"Um, hello? *I'm* a passenger, and I already have plenty of reason to be upset, thank you very much."

But if Gordon even heard her, he made no indication. Instead he gestured for someone behind her to come forward. At first she thought he meant Amani or one of the newlyweds, but as she turned around she was again faced with Lundgren.

"You bastard," Quinne hissed at him under her breath.

"Gordon, what do you want?" Lundgren asked.

"Can you give these four a hand heading back to where they can wait for the rescue?"

The message was clear. Gordon didn't want them interfering with the better-off passengers when it came time for the choppers. Maybe, if there was room in one of them after all these others had gotten aboard, someone from their group might be able to join them. Quinne wasn't going to sit around and wait for it, though.

"Don't touch me," Quinne said as Lundgren tried to take her elbow. "I can figure out what's going on for myself. And I sure as hell don't want to be around you any longer than I have to."

"If you're still pissed about what happened on the other side of the boat, lady, then get over. Nature voted and that woman died."

"Oh, fuck off so much," Quinne said. She turned to walk away, stopping only when it sounded for a second like Lundgren might be threatening one of the others, but he had already gone off and was gruffly directing the various groups of passengers where they should wait.

"So, what? Is that it?" Amani asked.

"Honey, I'm sorry to say this," Quinne said. "But I think it is.

I honestly think we're going to die today.

# CHAPTER TEN

They never were able to get a straight answer as to what or where the smoke was coming from, although the general speculation seemed to be that it had something to do with why the *Lucky Lady Duck* had come to a full stop. Whatever it was, the smoking stopped shortly before the brief night was over, and when the sun "came up," as in it no longer touched the horizon, Quinne's mind tried to tell her that it had to mean that this whole nightmare was over. Wasn't there old song about a morning after some disaster on a cruise ship? Whether there was or wasn't, the idea of a fresh start with a brand new day was purely an illusion. It was still the wee hours of the morning, and every single person aboard the ship was exhausted.

All the crazy panic seemed to have gone out of everyone, replaced with a vigilant sort of weariness. Most of the people still didn't seem to understand anything of what had happened, just that disaster had struck, and whatever leadership there was supposed to be on the ship was nowhere to be found. A few people came up to Quinne's group asking if they knew anything about what had happened and if there was going to be a rescue, at which point Quinne, Amani, and the newlyweds had been forced to make a decision. They could tell the truth of everything they knew, and probably do their part in starting a new wave of panic, or they could feign ignorance. Most of the time they chose to pretend not to know more than little tidbits: that there was indeed something dangerous in the sea, that something bad had happened to the captain, that someone somewhere had stepped up and was organizing a rescue. It was enough to make people cautious yet not lose so much hope that they might start doing stupid things that could put others in jeopardy. Many people had retired back to their rooms to quietly await some kind of word, and everyone now kept their distance from anything that overlooked the water when they could help it.

Quinne, Wanda, and Jimmy, however, had no desire to go back to their rooms. Even on the off chance that someone had put something over the gaping holes in the side of the ship, they all agreed that if they happened to go there and *not* get attacked again, they wouldn't be able to deal with the inevitable sight of blood in the hallway that had once been at least two people. With the area around the deck far too cold for them to stay out for much longer, they instead huddled together inside the main rotunda, taking a seat against wall outside a trendy little coffee shop that didn't look like it would ever open again. Amani could have headed back to her own room, which was a little economy-class thing not anywhere near any of the scenes of carnage, but she opted to stay with them. Grabbing some towels from the coffee shop, Wanda and Jimmy did their best to create a makeshift set of pillows and curled up with each other for a fitful rest. Quinne wished she could do the same, but every time she closed her eyes she thought she felt a jolt, like the wall next to her was caving in again and a serpentine head would pop through to snack on her. Amani seemed to be having similar trouble, so the two of them moved far enough away from Wanda and Jimmy that they could quietly converse without disturbing them.

"Yeah, so, this isn't exactly the most romantic or erotic hookup I've ever had," Quinne said. "Can't say I've been bored, though."

"I would have preferred boring, actually," Amani said.

"Can't really fault you on that."

They fell into an uneasy silence for several minutes. During all the chaos it had been easy to forget that they had only met a short time earlier, and even then they hadn't intended for the relationship to be anything other than a single night of sex. Running back and forth, trying to escape dangers, trying to find out what was going on, the two of them had felt like an inseparable pair that belonged together. Now, without the outside stimulation, Quinne was forced to remember that she didn't know anything about this girl, and they didn't actually mean anything to each other. It felt strange and a little sad.

"I didn't bring my smartphone with me for this trip," Quinne said. "Did you say earlier that yours is in your room?"

"Yeah," Amani said. "Why?"

"And lots of people should have their phones, correct? So there's no way what's happening hasn't been posted all over social media, right?"

"The ship has Wi-Fi and a signal and all that, but my experience with it has been spotty. I think it depends on the exact position of the ship. Anyway, we don't have any idea on the state of the communications equipment at this time. Or power. Have you noticed the way the lights seem to be flickering more and more?"

"Yeah, although I guess I've been trying to ignore it. So are you saying that you don't think people out in the rest of the world know what's happening?"

"Honestly, I think what the world knows about what's happening here has more to do with whether or not there's been a recent celebrity breakup. If something like that is trending, then no one would be paying attention to something like this anyway."

"That's a rather bleak view. Although, I suppose I know it's true. I am the one here who makes her money by showing off her naughty bits on the internet."

"Still, even with all that, someone else must have seen what's going on and sent some kind of rescue, right? Those three helicopters can't be it."

"I don't know anything about rescue procedures at sea, but I'd expect that part of the procedure would be to send rescue boats."

"That's good, right?"

"Think about it for a second, Amani."

She did, and Quinne watched the realization dawn on her face. There were at least two sea monsters out there, maybe more. Those two alone had managed to rip through a large cruise ship and bring it to a screeching halt. Unless the Canadian or Russian Navies were sending their largest possible ships, they likely wouldn't last long against the things prowling around in the ocean.

"But shouldn't the Navy and things like that be on high alert after what happened at Baja? I mean, before I came on this cruise I even thought I heard a rumor about something in the Galápagos Islands. It's almost like something's going on out there, and this is just another part of it."

"Just because all the scientific evidence clearly shows that it's happening doesn't mean that people are going to believe it. Hell, remember, there are actual, honest-to-god people out there who refuse to even believe dinosaurs existed. Get enough of those people in the right positions of power, and suddenly you get a crisis like this where they refuse to take it seriously. Whoever they called to help probably doesn't actually think we're being attacked."

Amani snorted. "And if they do, the assholes probably automatically assume that it's caused by people like me."

"You know, I think that's actually the first time I've heard you swear all night. At least in English. I think I even heard you say 'oh fudge' earlier."

"Yes, well, you can thank my parents for that. Even when I don't want to obey them anymore, I still find myself going into the old patterns that they taught me."

Quinne paused, wondering if this was really the right time to start digging into the enigma that this young woman presented. Then she figured it wouldn't hurt. If she didn't find out more about her now, they would both likely be too dead to have this conversation later.

"May I ask why you're here without them?" Quinne asked. "Or without anyone at all?"

"What, I can't go on a vacation alone? You did it."

"Yes, well, you don't really seem like the type. You're very simple and likeable. I can't imagine that it would be hard to get someone else to go along with you."

"I guess I could have invited friends, but really I just needed time to get away and think. You know, about things."

"Things like whether or not you want to sleep with women?"

Amani paused for a long time. "Yeah, I suppose that's part of it. But maybe not all of it. I'm pretty religious. It's been driving me nuts that I haven't been able to do any of my prayers or devotions while we've been so busy running for our lives. But I don't agree with people who say Allah would hate me if I was... if I turn out to be..."

"A lesbian?"

"Or bisexual. I guess I'm still trying to figure that out. But I know I'm not straight, and I have the distinct impression that I don't have any choice. It's just who I am, and I can't change it, whether my parents would disown me or not."

"So they don't know?"

"I think they suspect. A few of my siblings, too. I'm not so concerned about most of them, but I have no doubt that if I tell my parents that I'm attracted to women, they will refuse to ever see me again. So that's why I'm here, alone. I thought a cruise to the Arctic would be cool, and a Letroix cruise specifically would be fun, and it would give me time to think. That was stupid of me, though. With the political climate the way it is, the bigots have been out in full force and are in a hurry to scapegoat a Muslim girl traveling alone."

Quinne wanted to say that she understood, but that would be a lie. She knew she couldn't understand, not really. She had some experience getting treated like crap because of her sexual orientation, but it was a different type of crap than what Amani had to deal with. No, that wasn't completely true, Quinne realized. Amani would have to deal with homophobes now. She would just have to deal with it on top of religious bigots. Any attempt for Quinne to say something in comfort would probably come out privileged and asinine.

So Quinne did the only other thing she could think of. She scooted closer to Amani and put an arm around her shoulder. Amani tensed for a moment, and Quinne was fully prepared to let her pull away with no hard feelings, but after a few seconds Amani softened and leaned into Quinne's side. They were quiet again for a time before Amani said anything.

"What about you? There has to be a story for why you're here."

"Nope. No story. I just needed a vacation."

"On a Letroix Cruise, though? You'll excuse me if someone like you seems out of place among all the wholesome families."

"Hey, I'm wholesome. I'm wholesome as fuck. I'm so wholesome I can fit whole things into many holes."

"Oh wow. Porn puns. You must be getting loopy from lack of sleep."

"No, not that loopy. I have a tendency to make bad jokes when I'm nervous."

"It also seems like you're trying to get away from the question of why you're here. If you don't want to talk about it either, just tell me to back off. I'm okay with it."

"Really, there's nothing to tell." Quinne paused. She knew that wasn't really true, but her story wasn't anywhere on the same level as Amani's. Still, it was *her* story to tell, and Amani seemed interested, so she didn't see why not. "The thing you've got to know is that I'm proud of what I do. I'm not ashamed. There's nothing wrong with doing sex work of my own free will, and I don't take well to people who try to act like I'm in some precarious situation and need to be saved from myself."

"I don't think that at all."

"But what *do* you think about why I do what I do?"

"Uh, I guess I don't really think much of it at all. I've seen your vids, but I guess…" Amani paused, and Quinne could tell she was going to say something that anyone else might have found embarrassing. Quinne gently nudged her, indicating that she wouldn't judge. "I guess I haven't ever thought about who you might be other than a series of images to look at while I play with my vibrator."

"You don't need to be ashamed about that, you know."

"I know. I'm not ashamed about, you know, masturbation. I'm ashamed that I've never really thought of you as a human, I guess. It's different when I'm here talking to you."

"All of a sudden I'm more than just heavily tattooed skin?"

"Yeah."

"Well, I guess that's why I'm here. I'm here because sometimes I need to be reminded of that myself."

"Reminded of what?"

"That I'm human. That I'm not just there on the computer screen purely for others' pleasure. Okay, now don't get me wrong at all. I love what I do. But everyone always expects me to not just be Quinne, but be *the* Quinne Quiver, owner of a rapidly growing erotic media company, skinny and kinky little bitch unafraid to do anything and everything on camera provided it's legal in the state where I'm filming. But maybe sometimes I want a break from everyone else's expectations. Sometimes I just want to go on a damned cruise and smile like an idiot while I get my picture taken with…"

Tears ran down Quinne's cheek. Oh hell, was she really going to do this?

"Your picture taken with what?" Amani asked gently.

"Ever since I was a kid, watching the cartoons on TV, I just wanted to have my picture taken with someone dressed in that stupid Lucky Lady Duck costume."

"Oh."

There wasn't a lot to say after that, Quinne figured. And she didn't want to talk about her piddly little problems anymore, anyway. Except maybe for one thing.

"Sooo… I guess this just comes back to where we started the night," Quinne said.

"What do you mean?"

"I mean we have nothing to do but wait, either to get rescued or for the ship to sink, or maybe get eaten."

"Those are happy thoughts."

"Right. So if this indeed our last hours on Earth, shouldn't we spend them doing something other than sitting here?"

"Oh. Um. Right." Amani thought about it for a second, then stood up and offered Quinne a hand up. "Normally I think this is where I would ask your place or mine, but since yours is kind of out of the question, I guess we're going to mine."

# CHAPTER ELEVEN

"I'm kind of waiting for you to do that cliché thing," Amani said.

"Which thing?"

"The one where you ask if I'm okay, as though you're afraid you might have hurt me."

"Don't be silly. I know I didn't hurt you. You didn't ask me to."

"Har har."

"Do you *want* me to ask you that?"

"I don't know. Maybe. Sure. Go ahead."

"Are you okay?"

Amani had finished getting dressed again, and adjusted her headscarf in a mirror by her bed. Quinne was still naked, although they should probably get moving if they hoped to return to Jimmy and Wanda before they woke up. Quinne and Amani had left them a hastily scrawled note on a napkin, but given the state of things the newlyweds might still get worried. Not that Quinne or Amani really owed either of them any explanation, but given all the four of them had been through and seen tonight, it had only felt right not to worry them.

"It's kind of nice," Amani said.

"What is?"

"Someone asking me that. The first guy I ever did anything with didn't."

"So I'm guessing that just because I was your first woman

doesn't mean I was your first overall?"

"Yes. I mean no. I mean, there was some fooling around, but whether or not it was actually sex probably depends on how you define it. But anyway, it was at a school dance. He ran off pretty soon after because we almost got caught. Wouldn't even look at me for the rest of the night, and any attempt I made to talk to him afterward was really awkward." She gave Quinne a worried glance. "Is that what's going to happen here?"

"Avoiding you wouldn't really be an option at this point, even if I wanted to. And I definitely don't want to. I do kind of feel like you didn't answer the question, though." Quinne finally sat up and started hunting around for her underwear. She found the plain back panties twisted up in some of Amani's blankets, although she wasn't quite sure yet where her bra was.

"What question?"

"Are you okay? And you know I don't mean physically."

"I... I don't know." Amani leaned against the wall near the door and watched Quinne slip her underwear on. "I feel like I'm supposed to feel different. I kind of don't."

"Only kind of?" Quinne finally found her bra but didn't put it back on right away. She enjoyed the way Amani kept staring at her.

"Yeah, it's like, something's changed, but the change isn't anywhere near to being over yet. Like if something really mind-blowing happens to you, it takes a while for it set in that your whole reality has been altered."

*Kind of like being attacked on a cruise ship by prehistoric dinosaurs*, Quinne thought, but she didn't say it. Amani deserved to have this moment without any snark. Besides, Quinne thought she had had her own moment like that one, the thing that had happened with her uncle in the park when she was a teenager. But that was a memory she always tried to suppress, and it wasn't appropriate to bring it up here.

And yet Quinne couldn't resist going without comment completely. "Mind-blowing, huh? Good to know I've still got the touch without a camera recording me."

"Well, maybe that's not the right word. It was… different. Not at all like I expected."

"But did you like it? Are you going to regret this, if we somehow get out of this alive?"

Amani gave Quinne an appreciative look up and down. "Yes. I liked it. And no, no matter what happens after this, I don't think I'll regret it. And you better get the rest of your clothes back on before I decide not to regret it some more."

As much as Quinne would have had fun taking her up on that, she was very much aware that the time for any sort of fun was over. They'd had a brief respite to remind themselves that they were still alive, that they weren't like the boy in the hall or Becky going over the railing or Sarah in the Lucky Lady Duck suit. They existed, they were alive, and life could be beautiful. Now it was time to go back to trying to stay that way.

"Did you notice the lights flicker while we were…" Quinne paused, trying to think of the right way to characterize what they'd just done. It had been a little too personal to simply call it sex, but not quite intimate enough to say that it was making love. "…enjoying each other's company? And no, that's not a commentary on how good it was."

"No, I think you're right. The lights did flicker once, I think. Although I guess I can't be sure. I was distracted."

"Then we should get back to Wanda and Jimmy before the power fails completely."

While it had been easy to ignore the increasing foreboding on the ship while they were in Amani's room, it became impossible as they opened the door onto the hall.

"Oh, gross!" Amani said. "What the fudge is that smell?"

"Smells like sewage. The plumbing system must have failed."

Indeed, before they could walk very far down the corridor their feet were soaked, and most definitely not with sea water. There was a yellowish-brownish tint to it that Quinne really didn't want to think about, and at one point Amani said she thought she stepped in something muddy. Whether it was a blessing or a curse, the lights in the hall failed completely except for the emergency floodlights, which no longer gave them all the details of what they might be walking through.

The lights in the main rotunda were still working, although intermittently. It probably wouldn't be long until they failed, too, and if the cavernous space went dark Quinne wouldn't have been surprised to find a full-out riot beginning. Although, it looked like something similar might have already started. Many of the people who had camped out in here were headed for the exit with varying degrees of urgency. Quinne and Amani went to where they had last seen the newlyweds, but for nearly a minute they couldn't find them. Finally Wanda and Jimmy came out of the abandoned coffee shop. From the way the two of them were adjusting their clothes, Quinne figured they had probably woken up with the same idea as her and Amani.

"There you guys are," Jimmy said. "We were starting to worry."

"We, uh, we decided that, if we weren't sure we were going to make it through the night, we wanted some time in private." It suddenly occurred to her that this might be too much information, that Amani wouldn't want anyone else to know, and Quinne turned to her, worried that Amani would be disapproving. Amani certainly had a look on her face, although Quinne wouldn't have characterized it as disapproving or angry. It might have almost been relief, although the play of emotions across her face was much too complex to read completely accurately. Amani held out her hand and offered a small smile. Quinne took it without hesitation.

"Yeah, I guess I can see that," Jimmy said, although he kept his face neutral. Quinne couldn't be certain exactly what he thought, but neither did she really care. What she and Amani did together was their business.

"Any idea what's going on?" Quinne asked.

"No clue," Wanda said. "As soon as we heard people rushing for the exits, we... uh... um..."

"Wanda, I do porn. You don't need to be coy with me."

"Um, okay. We stopped with the sex and put our clothes back on. We know probably exactly as much as you two do."

"Maybe it's the rescue choppers," Amani said.

"Maybe," Quinne said. "I guess we'll just have to go see for ourselves."

On their way out they passed Masterson, along with the woman Quinne had seen him with earlier in the evening. They were in an over-exaggerated embrace, the kind Quinne might have expected to see done as a dramatic painting on the cover of an old VHS box. All that was missing was the woman clutching him by the leg instead of around the chest, and a massive, masculine sword in Masterson's hand.

"Don't go!" the woman said. "I... I love you!"

"Denise, thank you, but you can never be my first love. My first love will always be... SCIENCE!"

As the foursome left Masterson and his lady friend behind, Amani made a point of looking down at the soles of her feet.

"Something wrong?" Quinne asked.

"I guess not. It's just that I could have sworn we were wading through bullshit again."

They intercepted one family once they were back out on the deck who told them that they'd heard something about the lifeboats, but beyond that they didn't have any details. Quinne had a very bad feeling about that as they went back in the direction of Masterson's earlier conference for the better-off passengers. The closer they got, the more apparent it was that things had certainly been happening while the two couples had been getting busy.

Lundgren was here with the majority of his security force, or at least, Quinne assumed, the ones that were left. Several of their uniforms were torn and bloody, and their faces had a haunted and perplexed cast. Like so many other things tonight, Quinne was sure there was a story there. It just wasn't part of her story, so she would likely never find it out.

Those who didn't look like they had already been through hell were following Lundgren's orders as he informed the growing crowd to stay back. Beyond this line of security Quinne saw a great many of the passengers who had been here earlier, and all of them were crowding around the lifeboats. Mickey and Gordon were frantically going among them, looking like they were trying to talk the passengers out of something.

"What's going on?" Quinne asked the nearest man. He was in a Letroix Corporation uniform that identified him as a member of the cleaning staff.

"What, you asking me?" the man asked.

"Why? Should I not?"

"No, go right ahead, but nobody tells me anything. All I know is that the rich people seem to have gotten it into their head that they need to take the lifeboats."

"Why, is the ship sinking?" Jimmy asked.

"Again, how the hell am I supposed to know? To these people I'm little more than soulless furniture."

Quinne pushed through the growing crowd, making sure that she didn't lose track of her friends (which was still a strange way to think of them after so little time, she knew, but at this point it certainly felt true) among the jostling. Lundgren saw her and immediately pointed a Taser in her direction. "Don't you dare."

"Dare what?" Quinne said. "I don't have the slightest clue what's going on."

"These people are going to take some of the life rafts out and get to safety."

Quinne's jaw dropped. "Are you people fucking high?"

A very prim and proper looking man on the other side of the security team turned to Quinne with a look of disgust. "Don't swear. This is a family ship."

"Jesus Christ, would you people stop with the freaking out about swearing?" Quinne said. "People have died tonight, and probably a lot more will if you go out there in those tiny little things, but you're seriously stuck on whether or not I say the word fuck? Get your fucking priorities straight, you fucking dipshit!"

Mickey did his best to find a position that made him look taller. "Everyone listen! People have died tonight, and a lot more still will if any of you go out there in these tiny little boats."

Quinne through her hands up in the air. "That's literally what I just said!"

Jimmy nudged her. "Not literally. I kind of think stuck-up people like this are pretty much incapable of acknowledging that anything in the world might be more than PG-13."

Several of the people who had been working to set the boats up to lower stopped to look at Mickey. Most of them continued to ignore him, just like they ignored Quinne and the growing crowd.

"Look, I don't know what your game is, but you're not fooling any of us," a woman of about fifty said to Mickey. "There's no such thing as sea monsters. We'll be fine. In fact, we'll be better off out there than we will on here with all the overflowing sewage."

"How can you still not believe us?" Mickey said. "There's evidence of sea monsters all up and down this boat! You even saw the tooth Masterson found earlier!"

"It's a hoax," another woman yelled. "We're not idiots."

"Oh my God," Quinne muttered. "I think my brain is totally melting from the stupid."

"I guess sometimes people can't acknowledge the horror in the world if it hasn't happened to them," Amani said. "If you hadn't seen the plesiosaurus and the liopleurodon with your own eyes, would you believe it?"

"No. I'd probably be asleep in my room. I'm a heavy sleeper."

"But you're not asleep. You're awake with us. So what are we going to do about it?"

Quinne stared at her for several seconds before turning to Lundgren. "You've seen at least one of the creatures. You know those people won't last long if they go out there. You can help us save them from themselves."

"I didn't see shit, little girl."

"Language!" one of the wealthy passengers yelled at him as they climbed into the boat. The lifeboats were now on their pulley systems and each one was ready to be lowered into the water.

"Are you kidding me, Lundgren? You know exactly what that monster did to Sarah, er, I mean that woman that fell over the side."

Lundgren's stand-offish demeanor faded somewhat at that. "Just keep back, Miss Quiver. Nothing you or I do is going to convince these guys that they can't do this."

"You recognize me?"

"Uh, I, um, used to have a subscription. Before, you know, I found a place where I could get videos of you for free."

"Oh, nice. Just when I thought you couldn't be more of a douchebag."

Lundgren looked over his shoulder as the multiple boats began to lower over the side. "It's too late now, anyway."

Wanda gently touched her shoulder. "It was always too late, Quinne. Those people in those boats, they've never had to fight for anything in their lives. Everything has always been handed to them. They think that mortal danger is going without phones or internet for a couple hours."

"Look, all of you, just back away, alright?" Lundgren said. Quinne had to give him at least a small amount to credit. His voice cracked as he spoke. When he looked down at the boats halfway to the water again, she saw the one thing about this that must have upset him: Quinne hadn't seen it before, but some of those people had children with them. The youngest she could see was a toddler, all the way up to mid-teens. The oldest kid, probably only fourteen, looked back up at Quinne, and she could see the sheer terror in his eyes. His parents or his grandparents or whoever had forced him into this boat might be totally oblivious, but he knew. These folks were forcing him to his death.

"Lundgren, if you don't stop this, I will," Quinne said.

"And how exactly do you expect to do that?" Lundgren asked.

Quinne sighed. "This would be a lot easier if I just had a gun." She unzipped her coat, then muttered at Amani, Wanda, and Jimmy. "Get ready. I'm going to do the thing again."

"You know, I'm starting to think that should be used like a nuclear option," Wanda said. "You know, last resort only. It's just too powerful."

"What are you talking about?" Lundgren said. Quinne had to smile at the way he was suddenly backing away from her, short and skinny little thing that she was.

"This," Quinne said, lifting her shirt and bra up and aiming at the other security guards. Most of the men reacted with dropped jaws. One of the men, though, gave her a raised eyebrow that clearly said "Oh honey, you don't have anything I want under there." There were three women among the guards as well, two of whom looked disgusted that Quinne would use her assets in such a blatant way while the third was clearly pleased by what she saw.

All of them, at least, were either staring or glaring at the sight of Quinne's bare, tattooed chest. None of them noticed as Wanda, Amani, and Jimmy snuck through the crowd around them and made it to the electronic controls lowering the boats into the water.

They did notice, however, when the motors lowering the boats reversed and started bringing the lifeboats back up.

There was a collective cry of dismay from the boats, but Quinne didn't get a chance to go to the side and see anything. One of the female security guards came up beside her and cold-cocked her before Quinne could understand what was happening. For the next several seconds she was so dazed that she didn't register more than random images and noises. Someone, probably the guard that had hit her, yelled, "Bitch, show a little self-respect!" Quinne fell to her knees and the crowd around her went into chaos mode, people rushing back and forth and screaming and shouting, more guards telling Amani and the newlyweds to stop what they were doing…

Oh, and there was something that appeared to be a giant rat. Quinne would have just dismissed that as a hallucination caused by having her bell rung, if it hadn't triggered some recent memory.

Then there was just horrible pain in her arm. She was on the deck, unaware how she had gotten there but fully aware that something was wrong with her. She must have screamed or something, because she heard Amani's voice, sounding distant, calling her name. The time that passed could have been seconds or hours before a petite pair of hands grabbed her from behind by the armpits and tugged. Quinne blacked out for a few seconds more, then came back to something like her senses when she was once again able to see the sky. She hadn't even realized until now that the view had been blocked by the riot of passengers around her. Several passengers cried out as they were tasered, but the most notable sound was the cry of a child. That should have caused Quinne to cringe, but for now it meant that the child in question wasn't dangling like bait over the water.

"Ow. Whuh? Huh-whu-pen?" Quinne asked.

"Just, quiet, okay?" Amani said gently in her ear. "You're hurt."

"Mah urm. Ih hurz."

"It's broken. No, you probably don't want to look at it. Don't…"

Through sheer habit of doing the exact opposite of what she was told, Quinne looked at her arm, then immediately looked away. Considering it looked like she had an extra elbow, it was surprising that it didn't actually hurt more. That would likely be from shock. Once the pain finally hit her full force, it would be excruciating.

"I'm pretty sure someone trampled it," Amani said. "I reeeeeally don't think you should try moving it."

"Wunda? Jimmuh?"

"Wanda pulled Jimmy off to the side somewhere. I didn't see exactly where. It looked like someone kicked the sugar out of him."

"Shih. Iz okay. You kin swear."

"Fine then. Kicked the shit out of him. I think it was Lundgren, but then Lundgren also went after some of the people in one of the boats, so I don't really know. Everything's a mess."

"Okay, everyone shut the fuck up and sit the fuck down!" Lundgren said. He had a handgun out again and was pointing it in the air where everyone could see.

"Language!" someone called out to him.

"And the next person who acts like the word 'fuck' is the worst thing that could happen is going to get a bullet between the eyes. Is that fucking clear?"

There were murmurs, most of them saying that he wouldn't dare, but slowly, in a wave that passed through the crowd, everyone went silent and hunkered down.

Lundgren, keeping his gun where everyone could see it, went around to all of his security staff that were still standing and whispered instructions to them. A few of them were knocked out on the ground or injured, although none of the injuries seemed to be worse than scratches and bruises. Several of the passengers, however, had injuries similar to Quinne's, and many of them were definitely going to need a medic sooner rather than later.

All of it would have seemed like a waste, except every one of the boats was back up at the deck, and most of them were empty. A few still held an obstinate couple of people, but the few kids Quinne had seen were now back on the deck. She wasn't sure if she had really done a good thing or not. Maybe she had just delayed some of these people's inevitable deaths. She felt a small amount of satisfaction anyway, even though that was hard to concentrate on, considering the shooting pain growing in her arm.

"Okay," Lundgren said when he turned back to the subdued crowd. "Under normal circumstances, I would arrest ever single last one of you assholes. But we don't have the time or the room to round every one of you up. Instead, you are all going to disperse. No one is leaving in the life boats right now. We will keep them ready just in case, but it's far more dangerous out there than most of you…"

There was a sound, rather faint, but Quinne still managed to hear it through Lundgren's announcement. "Wait," she croaked. "Someone's still…"

She didn't think she was loud enough, but other people inevitably heard the same noise as her. They turned in the direction of the lifeboats, and Quinne finally saw that she had been wrong. Not all the lifeboats were where they were supposed to be. Someone was still manually lowering one into the water.

Lundgren realized he didn't have everyone's full attention, then looked in that direction. "Oh son of a bitch," he said.

Although the remaining guards tried to keep the crowd from moving, most of the people followed Lundgren as he went to the railing and looked over the edge.

"Help me up," Quinne said to Amani. "Need to see."

"Quinne, we need to get you to a doctor or a medic or…"

"Need to see," she said again. She tried to get up by herself, but accidentally put some weight on her broken arm. Her eyesight shot full of lightning, the agony hitting her other senses before she even properly registered it as pain.

"Okay, stop that!" Amani said. "I'll help you up if you stop being a stubborn idiot."

"Can't," Quinne barely managed to say. "That's me."

The two of them found a place with fewer people where they could look over the edge. Quinne braced herself to see some family of four lowering themselves to their doom. The parents were dressed strangely, though, and the two kids were abnormally hairy.

"What even are those things?" Amani asked.

"Capybaras," Quinne said, finally remembering why the possibility of giant rats had rung a bell.

"What's a capybara?" one of the other bystanders asked.

"A large rodent native to South America," someone else said. "They're herbivorous, and tend to keep to areas where…"

"It's Troid and Murga," Quinne interrupted.

"Who?" Amani asked.

"The magicians. The ones the Letroix Corporation booked as entertainment on the cruise."

"Oh, you think I could get their autograph?" someone in the crowd asked.

"Where's my camera phone?" someone else asked. "I need to get a picture of this."

That was why they were dressed so strangely. The two aging magicians were wearing their trademark red business suits, which they claimed they wore so that no one would see any blood on them in case something went wrong. That excuse might have once made sense in the early days of their act, but Quinne couldn't be sure what a capybara might do to someone to make them bleed. Maybe mistake them for a shrub and gnaw on them.

"What are those idiots doing?" a familiar voice said from behind Quinne. She turned to see Wanda holding onto to Jimmy as the two of them made their way to join her and Amani. Jimmy had a cut on his head and looked about as dazed as Quinne, but even with that he was still together enough to wince in sympathetic pain at the misshapen sight of Quinne's arm.

"They're making a break for it," Quinne said.

"Shouldn't someone try to stop them?" someone in the crowd asked. Quinne immediately saw, though, that any such effort would be wasted. The boat was almost down on the water. The two magicians would be able to detach the ropes before anyone could start hauling them back up.

"Shouldn't something be attacking them by now?" Wanda asked.

"Maybe we were wrong," Quinne said. "Maybe the creatures are gone. Maybe they'll be safe."

"Do you really think that?" Amani asked.

"No. I actually think they're dinosaur food. Those red suits might as well be ketchup."

Although there was a lot of angry and impatient murmuring among the people who had tried to escape in the boats, no one made an effort to get back in one and join Troid and Murga down on the water. By unspoken agreement, everyone had apparently decided that they would be the canaries in the coal mine, the potential sacrifices to test if the way was truly safe. Quinne felt somewhat guilty for thinking in those terms, but only somewhat. In the end, no matter what happened, these two were grown adults who had made their own choices. If anything, Quinne was more worried for the safety of the capybaras.

Troid and Murga undid the ropes on their lifeboat with the same flourish they would likely do anything in their act. Hell, maybe in their minds this really *was* part of their act. Watch the amazing Troid and Murga brave the unknown, a daring escape artist act for the ages! Kids, don't try this at home!

As if to prove this thought, the two magicians turned in the direction of the crowd up on the deck and took their bows. Strangely enough, there was a smattering of polite applause among their audience. Quinne herself might have given into the impulse if she didn't think clapping might make her pass out.

"You think they'll make it?" someone asked.

Quinne snorted. "Make it where? Do you people keep forgetting that we're in the middle of the Arctic? Best case scenario is that they end up on a melting ice floe with a starving polar bear." Still, Quinne couldn't help but root for them. There were various ports and supply areas around for situations just like this, right? It wasn't like they were the HMS *Terror*, where the ship had been forced to float into the unknown. This was the twenty-first century. There *was* no unknown anywhere left on Earth. Everything had been mapped and quantified.

*If that's true*, a little voice at the back of Quinne's head asked, *then how did we somehow manage to run into the first dinosaurs in millions of years*?

"Crap," she muttered to herself. "Those guys are screwed."

The lifeboat had both a motor and oars, but the oars were probably only intended as backup in case the motor failed. The capybaras had already discovered the oars and decided they were chew toys, anyway, so the magician duo had started up the motor and were already a respectable distance from the ship. Far out enough, in fact, that a number of the people around her had already begun murmuring that it was safe all along, that they should go too, that it would be better to be prepared in one of the lifeboats than being caught unaware if the ship sank. Under any other circumstances, Quinne might have agreed. But the images of the two monsters were still fresh in her mind. Which one would it be, Quinne wondered. The plesiosaurus had definitely been the more aggressive one, ripping right into the ship like it were tinfoil covering leftovers to snack on. The liopleurodon hadn't done anything until it was provoked, but would it consider Troid and Murga and their amazing capybaras to be invading its territory?

In the end, the correct answer was neither.

Lundgren, of all people, was the first person to notice the disturbance in the water. That was probably because everyone else's concentration was on the magicians in the lifeboat. Lundgren must have been scanning for threats, because he was one who said, "Look!" and pointed off farther to the south. At first Quinne would have guessed the sudden vortex of water was from the liopleurodon, except almost immediately afterward something emerged, and then kept emerging. It rose up out of the water, at first making Quinne think of a submarine coming to the surface. But as the object kept rising, she realized it was too tall, too thin, like a giant serrated tooth broken off from the Guinness Book of World Records's largest hacksaw.

It took a few seconds for the improbable sight to register for what it was, and as soon as it did a gasp swept through the crowd.

It was a fin. Huge and gray, definitely bigger than had ever been recorded on a normal shark.

"Holy shart," Amani said. Apparently she still couldn't just say the word shit, but Quinne gave her props for at least being somewhat vulgar this time. "It's just like that footage of the hammerhead down in Mexico!"

"No," Quinne said. "That's not the same shark."

"How do you know?"

"First, I don't know much about shark migrating patterns, but I doubt it would have swum all the way up to the Arctic. Second, I think that's much bigger. Think about it, Amani. We've have a plesiosaurus and a liopleurodon. What do you think would work next to continue with that theme?"

Amani thought about it for a moment before taking a deep breath. "Oh shit."

Quinne wanted to congratulate her foul mouth, but the horror show in front of them was just beginning to ramp up. Neither Troid nor Murga seemed to realize that something was coming up from behind their lifeboat. They were far enough away that Quinne couldn't see for sure, but their movements made them look like they were arguing. The capybaras, on the other hand, had started to get skittish. Murga turned to see what was wrong with the animals just as first one, then the other, leaped over the side of the boat.

"I didn't know capybaras could swim," Amani said.

"I still don't even know what a capybara is," someone else in the crowd responded.

The capybaras, of course, had dove over the edge as far from the approaching tsunami of freezing sea and prehistoric monster as they could, which meant that both Troid and Murga now completely had their backs to the approaching menace. Wanda started to scream, telling them to watch out, and the call was taken up by the rest of the passengers watching helpless from the ship. Whether because the two magicians heard them or because they finally registered the way their boat shook as the creature approached, the two of them turned around.

Quinne was sure the looks on their faces would have been something to behold, but the two men were too far away for anyone to see. What everyone on the *Lucky Lady Duck* could see, however, with no problem whatsoever, was the enormous monster out of nightmares that rose up from the sea. In many ways Quinne supposed it look like a great white shark, but only if the largest great white were actually this thing's tiny newborn offspring. It moved with lightning speed and efficiency, so much that if the crowd hadn't already been looking at the lifeboat they might have missed its final moments. The creature barely even needed to open its mouth for the two men and their little boat to easily slide into its gullet. As far as Quinne could see, there wasn't even any blood as it ate the two of them. It hadn't even needed to chew. It just opened up, swallowed, and then dove back down into the deep. The dorsal fin stayed visible to the crowd for several seconds before it too vanished, along with any clue that the two magicians had been there.

It was their last great disappearing act, yet nobody applauded. They probably would have been disappointed.

A few people here and there among the crowd screamed or cried out, but the rest of the group was surprisingly reserved. Quinne looked around and saw that most of the people had looks of resignation on their faces. Those few that hadn't believed what was happening certainly believed now, and those that had already believed had their worst fears confirmed: they were all going to die out here. There was no escape, at least not by boat.

"What was that?" Jimmy asked.

"A megalodon," Amani said.

"And I suppose that's from a YouTube video also?" Wanda asked.

"No, just kind of well known," Amani said. "The prehistoric predecessor to the shark, among the largest predators to have ever lived. There might have only been one or two things that were bigger."

A long, low, and mournful howl echoed out over the wind. Everyone in the crowd looked around for the source, but there was nothing to be seen. Quinne's best guess was that the sound had come from somewhere out in the sea. For something to be able to make that sound, over that kind of distance, Quinne guessed that it had to be big. And not just big like the things they had already seen. Big on a scale they couldn't yet understand.

"And do I even want to know what that was?" Jimmy asked.

"Probably not," Quinne said. "But if I had to guess, I'd guess what it was not. And that was probably not a plesiosaurus, a liopleurodon, or a megalodon. That was something else entirely."

# CHAPTER TWELVE

"Wait. Hold up. I'm not sure about this," Quinne said.

"What's not to be sure of?" Jimmy asked.

"Maybe we should wait and have a doctor take care of it."

"I'm sure there's plenty of doctors all over the ship, assuming they didn't somehow get eaten right along with the captain. But I'm telling you, you don't want to let this sit for too long. Just trust me. I know what I'm doing."

"But you're only a nurse!"

"Hey, you obviously don't know as much as you act like you do if you think there's ever such a thing as 'only a nurse.' And also? Probably not a good idea to insult the person holding your broken arm in his hands."

"It's just, is this going to hurt?"

"Probably. Definitely. I might even say extremely."

"Oh God."

Jimmy raised an eyebrow at her but lowered his voice so that only she could hear. Wanda and Amani were standing nearby, where they were watching all the other people trying to make preparations throughout the mostly darkened rotunda. What exactly they were trying to make preparations for, Quinne couldn't say, but it was human nature to try to do something even when there was nothing that could possibly be done.

"Quinne, seriously?" Jimmy asked. "This is not what I would expect from you."

"Why not?"

"Because I've seen some of your videos, remember? There's quite a few of them where you are in no shortage of pain."

"Yeah, but that's a good kind of pain. The fun kind."

"Don't you have some kind of technique you use if it gets to be too much?"

"Yeah, it's called a safe word."

"Heh. Well, I don't think that will stop much this time. Quinne, we have to do this now if you want any hope at all of ever being to use your arm properly again."

Quinne took a deep breath. "Okay. Fine. Do it on three."

"Okay. One…"

"Wait, wait, wait! You're not going to do that one thing, are you?"

"What thing?"

"The thing where you say you're going to do it on three but then you surprise me by actually doing it on two."

"That would be a dick thing for me to do. Unless that's actually what you *want* me to do?"

"Um, yeah, actually. Could you do that?"

"Doesn't that kind of defeat the point if you already know in advance that I'm doing it on two?"

"Just, just do it. Please. While I've got my nerve up."

"Fine. One. Tw…"

Halfway through the word Jimmy twisted the broken bone of her arm back into what was more or less the correct shape. Quinne screamed, although to her surprise the pain was far from the most excruciating she'd ever felt in her life. That honor still went to the time she'd done that specialty video for a rather wealthy client, the one where she and Manda Slaughter had needed a handful of thumbtacks and a cactus. Quinne took several quick breaths as her vision shot full of blue and white, then everything faded into a dull, ever-present and throbbing pain.

"You okay?" Amani asked her, stooping down next to Quinne

and putting a comforting hand on her shoulder.

"Fucking peachy keen," Quinne said. She made an effort to lift the broken arm, but doing anything more than letting dangle at her side was too painful. "So what now? Shouldn't I have a cast or a splint on this or something?"

"If you just sit tight here, I'll go see if I can find something," Jimmy said.

"I think there was some kind of janitor supply closet just around the corner," Amani said.

"Can you show me?" Jimmy asked. The two of them went off together, leaving Quinne to do her quivering (and again, not the good kind) on the floor with Wanda looking after her.

"So," Quinne said. "Hi."

"Um, hi?" Wanda said back.

"Haven't really had much of a chance to get to know each other so far, have we?"

"Is that really something we should be doing right now?"

"Do you have something better to do?"

"Guess not."

"So why this cruise?" Quinne asked.

"What do you mean?"

"I mean, you guys are newlyweds, right? Why a cruise to the Arctic? And one through the Letroix Corporation?"

"What, that isn't your idea of a honeymoon?"

"Well, I suppose there are plenty who would think so. Except if I ever get married, not that I expect to get married until I'm in my sixties or something, I'll probably spend my honeymoon in a BDSM dungeon."

"No, you wouldn't. That's something I've figured out about you so far. You like to talk like this super-worldly, over-sexed vixen, but there's a definite softer side."

"Okay, fine. If you really want to know, I plan to take my eventual honeymoon at the Wizarding World of Harry Potter. But that's beside the point. What are *you* doing here?"

"Hey, it's not like we have a problem with this trip or anything. I was loving it, up until the point where a massive dragon-thing tried biting our heads off. But you're right. It wasn't our first choice. Everything about this trip was sort of last minute." Wanda shrugged in a way that almost came across as shy. "Including the wedding. We were only engaged for a month, and we knew each other for just six months before that."

"Talk about quick. Must have been love at first sight."

"I guess. But maybe it's more like... what do they call it when you fall in love with someone who's been taking care of you?"

"The Florence Nightingale Effect."

"Yeah, that's it. He was my nurse while I was in chemo. We fell in love. And then..."

Quinne suddenly had the feeling that she had stumbled into something more personal than she had been ready for. "And then what?"

"And then I stopped chemo."

"So your cancer went into remission? What kind was it?"

"Colon cancer. And no, it didn't."

It took Quinne half a second to get her meaning. "Oh. I see. Uh, I'm..."

"Don't. Everyone's sorry. I just assume that."

"Um, do you mind if I ask a few questions about it?"

"Normally I'd say yes I do mind, but honestly, what's the point in holding anything back anymore? Ask away."

"You... you don't look sick."

"There's lots of people with debilitating illnesses that don't look sick. That doesn't mean they're not struggling in ways you can't see."

"I guess, it's just... when I picture cancer patients..."

"You're seeing me on a good day. I may not be on chemo anymore, but I'm still taking various meds for the pain. I want to experience what I still can *while* I still can. I'm not going to a sick bed until I absolutely have to." Wanda actually chuckled. "I've kind of developed a thing with beds. I won't go anywhere near them if I can. Drives Jimmy nuts. We've had to get creative any time we want to get intimate."

"Jesus. So you two fell in love, got married as soon as possible, took the first cruise you could get, and whoops, got stuck in all this."

"Pretty much. Ironic, I know. Try to take every advantage of how much life I have left, and instead I end up cutting it shorter. And taking my husband down with me." She paused at that. "Husband. Still so weird to call him that. Before I went into chemo, I'd kind of assumed that marriage would just be a part of human existence I would never experience. But Jimmy was there. Sometimes I wonder if he's only there because he pities me."

"I don't know. It certainly looks like love to me," Quinne said.

Wanda gave her a sad smile. "Yeah, it really does sometimes, doesn't it?" They both saw Jimmy and Amani returning, with some kind of cord and a broken broom handle in Jimmy's hand. "You don't need to tell him that I said any of this, okay? Given everything that going on, I think we've both almost forgotten. Strange, yet it's nice."

"Lips are sealed," Quinne said. When Jimmy and Amani were back Jimmy did his best to use the broom handle as a splint, and while the cord was a terrible binding, it would at least work for the next one or two hours. And although none of them said it out loud, she could see it on everyone's faces: they all knew there were only a couple hours left. They were either going to get rescued, or else the monsters surrounding the ship would get tired of waiting for morsels to fall in the water. For all any of them knew, the ship could be slowly sinking with all the damage to it.

"Hey, look," Amani said, pointing to the center of the rotunda. Gordon and Mickey were there again, and it looked like they were setting up some kind of box for someone to stand on.

"Wait, weren't those two hanging around while those people were trying to get into the lifeboats?" Wanda asked. "What happened to them? It's like they just disappeared."

"Or else whoever was writing the script for this particular disaster movie completely forgot they were supposed to be there," Jimmy said.

"Don't be silly. It's obvious that those two and Masterson would be the main characters," Quinne said. "We're just background extras. The writer wouldn't forget about the two main sidekicks. And also, there's this whole thing where all of this is real and not a movie, in case you didn't remember."

Masterson strode in into the rotunda from somewhere, and again Quinne was reminding of an aging pro-wrestler who honestly didn't know how to act like anything *other* than a wrestler. He even had beautiful arm candy clinging to his side. The woman he had been talking with earlier stayed near him at all times. Judging from the messy state of her hair and deep flush of her cheeks, Quinne had an idea of what they two of them had been doing immediately before this.

"Huh," Wanda said.

"What?" Quinne asked.

"Looks like we're not the only ones who got busy tonight," Wanda said. "Who would have guessed that being almost eaten by sea monsters was such an aphrodisiac?"

Masterson stood up on the box Mickey and Gordon had provided for him, effortlessly stepping on it without looking like he'd practiced it, or else simply expected that there would always be some kind of stage for him to stand on and hold court no matter where he might go. "Okay, everyone, listen up!" Masterson ejaculated.

"Ejaculated again," Quinne said. "Seems to me like someone is getting lazy with their thesaurus."

"Or someone just thinks the word 'ejaculated' is inherently funny," Wanda added.

"Well yeah, who wouldn't?"

"We have had a bad day! We all know this!" Masterson ejected. "Everyone knows by now what's happening! Everyone has seen the dinosaurs in the water by now!"

From the way a number of the people murmured, Quinne guessed that a majority of the passengers had seen nothing of the sort, and most of them were still in denial that such a thing was possible.

"Wait, what is he doing?" Amani asked Quinne.

"My guess is this is supposed to be the big rousing speech before the final fight to survive."

"Quinne, how many movies do you actually watch that you keep thinking of things this way?"

"Not that many, I swear."

"...but this is the trait that has made us the dominant species on the planet!" Masterson continued expounding. "Our will to survive! And now, that trait is going to be..."

"Seriously, this sounds rehearsed," Jimmy said.

"Do you think maybe he was practicing while he was doing that bimbo over there?" Wanda asked.

"God, that would be a funny sight," Jimmy said. "Probably a little disturbing, too."

"... the last thing they ever did! That's what made the Romans so formidable!" Masterson erupted. "Even if they did get fruity in the bedroom, we should still omelet-late them for..."

"Oh for fuck's sake, seriously?" Quinne said. "Did the bastard really have to pull out the casual homophobia?"

"Probably doesn't even realize what he said was offensive," Amani said.

"Omelet-late?" Wanda asked. "Could someone please tell me what that's supposed to mean?"

"I think he meant 'emulate,'" Jimmy said.

"Okay, ever second I keep listening to this, I can feel my brain breaking down into its base elements," Quinne said.

"So here's what's going to happen!" Masterson enervated. "We're going to fight! We're going to survive! We're going to dine on the blood of..."

"What do you want to bet his speech tags have devolved to the point where they're nothing but random, meaningless words that begin with E?" Quinne asked.

"Nuh-uh. No more bets for me," Jimmy said. "I already owe you money I won't be able to pay before I die."

"Is there any real reason that we're still here listening to this?" Amani asked.

"Maybe he actually has important information he needs to tell us," Wanda said.

"Chocolate!" Masterson encumbered. "With a cherry on top!"

"Or not," Wanda said.

"Maybe it would be less annoying if we went back out on the deck?" Amani asked.

"We could wait and see if the helicopters are going to show up. They should be here soon, right?" Quinne asked. "If they're coming at all, that is. For all we know, all that talk was bullshit."

"Now here's the deal!" Masterson echo-located. "There are helicopters coming! There will only be three of them at first, but there will be more afterward! We have already come up with an intricate way of deciding who will get on the first ones..."

"Hell, actual information," Wanda said. "I'm almost impressed. Almost."

"Intricate way of deciding my ass. That's just his way of keeping people from freaking out that the higher-paying passengers get to go first," Quinne said. "Such bullshit."

"Wait, is anybody out there waiting for the helicopters right now?" Amani asked.

"Well, there's got to be, right?" Quinne asked. "It's not like they would have all just abandoned their spot out there…"

The four of them looked around themselves at the people gathered in the rotunda. From where they stood, it would have been easy to believe that nearly every person on the ship was here listening to every word Masterson electrocuted, or ennuied, or equidistanced, or whatever the hell he might be doing now. Quinne had stopped trying to figure it out. On a balcony looking down on Masterson, Quinne saw the asshole with the red trucker hat and his angry lady-friend, both of them staring slack-jawed at the man as though Masterson preached the word of God itself. Off to their right, she saw most of the people that had previously been fighting to get on the lifeboats. There were also a number of people in various Letroix Corporation uniforms, from the café staff to the janitors to the… well, whatever the hell other type of shit jobs people had to do on a cruise ship.

Everyone. In here. Listening.

"Guys? Back out very slowly," Quinne whispered to the others. "While everyone is distracted."

"Why are we whispering?" Jimmy whispered back.

"Because if the helicopters show up while this idiot has a captive audience, then we might actually have a chance at being on one of the first choppers out."

"I'm sure there's got to be others that we should help first," Jimmy said. "Injured people, children…"

"You're right. It's selfish of me to think otherwise. But how much do you think we're going to see that from these douchbags we saw trying to get into the boats earlier? We should get out there, now, where we can help the most. And maybe have a chance not to die today."

It would have been a good idea. It might have even helped them, as well as others, and possibly saved lives. Except that was the moment where they all ran out of time.

Something hit the ship. Whatever it had been, it was far bigger than any of the creatures they had seen thus far.

# CHAPTER THIRTEEN

The floor beneath everyone tilted as the entire huge cruise ship noticeably swayed with the impact. The rotunda was packed so full that some large pockets of people stayed upright simply because there was no room for them to fall, while in other places everyone toppled over. Quinne managed to keep her feet, although she almost fell over herself with the pain when Amani, unthinkingly trying to grab onto anything she could for support, took Quinne by the arm. Quinne thought Amani might have apologized, but the rotunda was full of confused screams and crying, drowning out everything except Quinne's panicked thoughts. Looking at the screeching, confused mass of humanity all around her, she realized this was probably the last place they wanted to be right now.

"Get out!" Quinne yelled to her companions. "Out on the deck!" In truth, she wasn't sure that would be a very safe place for them at all, but she had the feeling that no single place on the ship could be called safe anymore. Their best chance, then, was to not be in the middle of a crowd that was on the verge of stampeding, if they could only stand back up on the still-slanting floor.

Wanda and Jimmy had taken a tumble, but Wanda was up and helping Jimmy to his feet before either Quinne or Amani could assist them. Once they were out on the deck, the severe tilt of the ship was more noticeable, thanks to the distant horizon clearly not being parallel to the boards beneath their feet. It wasn't quite so slanted, though, that none of them would lose their footing. Or, at least, not yet. Another colossal bang hit the ship, and this time every one of the four toppled over. The hit had managed to set the *Lucky Lady Duck* back to being something more or less flat. However, although it easily could have been Quinne's imagination, once she stood back up she thought that the view of the water over the side was slightly closer than it had been before.

"Is the ship sinking?" Quinne asked.

The entire ship shifted again as it was hit with a wave that shouldn't have existed this far out to sea without a storm.

"I don't think the problem is that it's sinking," Jimmy said. "I think there's something going on over there off the uh, port side? Starboard side? I don't even know which is supposed to be which."

"Left," Wanda said, pointing in that direction. "Something's happening over on the left side."

"Do we even want to know?" Amani asked.

"At this point, I think that's kind of the same thing as asking if we want to have any chance at all of surviving," Quinne said. "Way too much has already happened that we don't have the details to."

That same mournful, ungodly loud moan that they'd heard earlier echoed out over the Arctic Ocean, only this time the volume made Quinne think that, whatever had made it, it was closer. As if in response, something hit the ship again, although not with quite the same devastating force that they'd felt earlier. Eager to know and yet at the same time not wanting to know at all, Quinne moved closer to the edge of the deck on the left side, taking every step carefully just in case the ship rocked violently underneath them again. They didn't have to go far before she could see the massive splashes and waves, and then just a little farther before their first view of the phenomenon. "Phenomenon" was about the only word Quinne's head could come up with to describe it at first, as she didn't have any sort of context with which to categorize it. Except perhaps in the movies. Or in wrestling. Maybe it was her association with Masterson as a failed pro-wrestler, but that was where she suddenly found the best contest.

This was a cage match, a royal rumble, or whatever the hell it was called when all the biggest wrestling name were in the ring together and all going at each other in a free-for-fall. This was Sea Monster Survival Series: The Pay-Per-View Event of the Year.

She could clearly see all three of the previously noted sea-dwelling dinosaurs. The megalodon was pacing the perimeter of a massive patch of sea, what Quinne was now stuck thinking of as the ring, while the plesiosaurus and the liopleurodon swam at each other and snapped and made hissing noises completely unlike any serpent she had ever heard before. The ring, unfortunately, seemed to share one whole side with the *Lucky Lady Duck*. The liopleurodon leaped and made an attempt at the plesiosaurus's neck, and the resulting disruption of the sea when it landed caused another wave to buffet the ship, shaking it slightly.

"Those waves," Amani said. "Are those what we keep hearing hitting the ship?"

"No," Quinne said. "I don't think so. I think those big bangs are when... incoming!"

As if to illustrate what she had just been about to say, the megalodon peeled off from its route and went for the liopleurodon. The liopleurodon was close enough to the ship that when it thrashed in an attempt to get out of the way, its tail smacked the ship. That caused a shudder significantly greater than the wave, but even that was not equal to the massive lurch the cruise ship had made the first time. Instead, they felt another one of those seconds later as the megalodon, its jaws wide open just like when it had swallowed Troid and Murga whole, rammed the liopleurodon, and the force of its hit smashed both creatures into the side of the ship. Quinne heard the horrible creaking of metal and breaking of plastics that signaled major damage to the side of the ship. The *Lucky Lady Duck* lurched again, worse than the first time, and Quinne, Amani, and the newlyweds all had to grab hold of something bolted down in order to keep from being flung over the side.

"That's not the same side as the first hit!" Jimmy said over the tortured squeal of parts of the ship giving way somewhere lower to the water. "Are there more than just these three on the other side?"

The three creatures answered that question for him. The plesiosaur darted off toward the back of the boat with a speed that Quinne would never have guessed from something so huge and awkward looking. The megalodon followed immediately after, and within a few seconds she could hear them fighting somewhere else. There didn't need to be more than just the three. They alone were fast and desperate enough to circle around the ship, putting the cruise ship directly in the center of their aquatic melee. The liopleurodon came into view a few seconds later and followed them, although at a significantly slower pace than before. It was hard to be sure, but Quinne thought she saw it trailing blood behind it.

"If this were a first blood match, then Leo would have already lost," Quinne muttered.

"Huh? What did you say?" Wanda asked.

"Nothing. Just losing my sanity."

"We need to get life jackets," Jimmy said.

"What good is that going to do?" Quinne asked. "If any of us falls in the water at this point, we aren't going to survive long enough to drown."

"Damn it, Quinne, listen!" Jimmy said. "Can't you hear that?"

The sounds of the fight, even as it moved again to the far side of the ship, were loud enough that at first she couldn't hear anything else. Then it came to her that the squealing of something vital failing in the ship beneath her hadn't stopped. The *Lucky*

*Lady Duck* might have been able to survive most of the earlier abuse it had suffered, but it was coming close to its limit.

"The ship's not going to last much longer, is it?" Quinne asked.

"We're all about to end up in the Arctic Ocean one way or the other," Jimmy said. "Our choices might very well be between maybe dying from getting eaten, or definitely dying of drowning."

"I suppose it wouldn't actually be very helpful if I pointed out that you're forgetting about hypothermia?" Wanda asked.

"No, honey, it wouldn't," Jimmy responded. The way he said it, though, was sweet, almost tender, as if this were just another of many minor tiffs they would have throughout their marriage, and they already were ready to laugh about it. He even leaned over and kissed Wanda's cheek. Quinne would have thought it cute.

If not for, you know, sea monsters and stuff.

"This way!" Amani said, pointing them in the direction of a nearby door. "If I remember the safety briefings, that's where the life vests should be."

By the time they had secured vests for each of themselves, more people had poured into the area. Whether they were here specifically for the life vests or they had just been running in a panic and decided that what these strangers were up to might be a good idea, they swarmed Quinne, Amani, Wanda, and Jimmy, frantically begging for life vests of their own. Quinne and the others did their best to help distribute them, trying to make sure that children and more vulnerable passengers had vests first, but it all devolved pretty quickly as the supplies in this particular cache of life vests dwindled. Many of the people moved on to the next place where they might find some, while the foursome escaped back inside through a service door. They found themselves in a plain corridor that the passengers were probably not intended to ever see, but which had numerous other doors that Quinne assumed led to other parts of the ship.

"Something tells me that wasn't the orderly emergency procedure pre-approved by the Letroix Corporation for these kind of situations," Wanda said.

"I don't think this situation was one that Letroix ever had an emergency plan for at all," Quinne said. "But I agree. You'd think that every single person on this ship, both the passengers and crew, had never in their life been told what exactly they were supposed to do on a cruise ship emergency. Somebody didn't do their research."

"No time to complain about implausibilities right now," Amani said. "We've got to figure out what we're going to do."

Another massive shudder sent all four of them slamming into the wall. The floor tilted at an angle again, and Quinne didn't think it would right itself this time.

"Anybody have any ideas?" Quinne asked.

"Don't look at me," Jimmy said. "My entire knowledge of what to do or not do in a nautical emergency comes from watching *Titanic*."

"God, I hate that movie," Quinne said. "So insipid."

"Hey." Jimmy looked legitimately hurt. "I love that movie."

"Oh please. It's three hours of Rose setting up Jack to murder him at the end."

"There wasn't enough room on the door!"

"There totally was!"

"No, if both of their weights had been on it, the buoyancy and balance would have been off, so…"

"Focus!" Amani yelled at them. "Stop bickering humorously like you're being written by Joss Whedon!"

"Yeah, I have to agree with that," Wanda said. "We all know what happens to the characters in a Joss Whedon show."

"Okay, fine," Quinne said. "So what do we do?"

There was a light shudder and a lurch. Quinne's stomach flipped like she was in an elevator that suddenly dropped an inch, then stopped.

"Higher ground," Jimmy said. "As far away from the water as we can get for as long as possible. That way we can avoid both being eaten and freezing to death. At least for now."

"As a plan, I have to say it lacks detail," Quinne said. "But I certainly don't have anything better. How about anyone else?"

Wanda and Amani shook their heads. Without any further words, Jimmy and Quinne led them in search of the nearest staircase or ladder or elevator, anything at all that might give them even a few more minutes of time before it would all end for them.

# CHAPTER FOURTEEN

They only ran into two other people in the service corridors. One was someone in a kitchen uniform who was curled up on the floor against the wall and crying into their arms. The foursome spent about a minute trying to convince the person to get up and follow them, but the person never even acted like they heard them. Quinne couldn't even guess at their gender, given the way the person kept their head and chest down and away from them, and the dim emergency lights of the corridor did little to help. Finally the group decided they couldn't afford to stay there any longer and left the person behind. Quinne filed the person away in her mind as Jess, quietly wishing Jess Godspeed and hoping for the best for them. The other person they only saw briefly from a distance. She looked like a teenage girl in a white dress who walked into the corridor, stared at them from a distance, then calmly walked off around a corner. When the foursome reached the corner, they saw no sign of her.

The entire experience would have been hideously quiet and eerie if only the ship around them hadn't kept shimmying and shaking. The floor had gradually been going at more and more of a slant, enough so that when they finally found a set of stairs leading up they found it difficult to go up them without clinging desperately to the railing. Amani made a comment that she thought she could hear rushing water somewhere farther down the stairwell, although Quinne didn't want to stop long enough to listen. If Amani was right, the rushing water could have just been a burst pipe somewhere. Or it could be a sign that the ship was really and truly sinking.

They would have gone all the way to the top, but the final door was locked and there appeared to be no way of opening it without a key. They had to go a couple of floors down to find an exit that would open for them. They came out on a long, open walkway that gave a spectacular view of the ocean.

"Where even are we?" Jimmy asked.

"As far as I can tell, the Letroix Corporation's equivalent of the penthouse," Quinne said. Nothing else about the ship as they had experienced had been run down or bad, but it was obvious that the cramped hallways and small rooms of their own floor were economy class. Here was the ritzy area. Well-tended plants were positioned at key areas to catch the sunlight (or at least they looked like they had been, before the ship had shifted and the pots had slid). Even though this whole walkway was open on one side, the place felt warm, heated from some hidden vents maybe. Probably incredibly wasteful, but that wasn't the kind of thing that people who could afford having rooms here would care about. The doors to the individual rooms were made of some kind of wood that Quinne couldn't even begin to hope to identify, although she had no doubt that the wood was real and not just some kind of particle board like their own doors.

Wanda let out a low whistle.

"I know, right?" Quinne said. "Given how much I had to pay just for my cheapo ticket, I can't imagine what it would cost to have a room up here."

"Okay, so now what are we going to do?" Jimmy asked. "We have higher ground."

"I… I don't know. Is anyone in any of these rooms?"

They knocked on two or three of the doors. Only once did they hear a voice on the other side, a woman who breathlessly told them that they needed to go away or else she was going to call the cops. Quinne wasn't quite sure how that was supposed to work in the woman's mind, but she didn't think trying to talk to her would accomplish anything. Otherwise most of the doors were locked. One opened at Amani's touch, showing a spectacular suite inside including a Jacuzzi, a complete fully stocked bar that looked like it needed to be manned by a real bartender servicing the occupants at all times, and something in the bathroom that none of the others could identify (although Quinne certainly knew a bidet when she saw one.) The room looked like it had been hastily abandoned, with a few socks and frilly panties still sitting on the floor in the bedroom. They found a few minor first aid supplies and spread them out among the four of them, just in case, but beyond that there was nothing in the room to help them.

In fact, there didn't seem to be anything on this entire floor to help them. Unless they suddenly decided their lives depended on playing a game of racket ball. A sign on the walkway said there was a court nearby.

"Okay, let's all just stop and take a breath," Quinne said. "Get our bearings, assess where we are, that kind of shit." Maybe the situation wasn't as dire as they had initially believed. The floor no longer seemed to be shifting beneath them, at least, and might have even gone back a little toward being level.

"Wait, when was the last time we even felt something hit the ship?" Jimmy asked.

"When we were about halfway up the stairs," Wanda said. "You think maybe those creatures have gone somewhere else?"

"Hmm" was all Quinne said. She didn't think anything of the sort, but she didn't want to be the pessimistic one. She would welcome an end to this madness just as much as anyone else. But realistically, if there was a calm, likely they were about to go through a final storm.

"Someone hold my hand?" Quinne asked.

Amani immediately took it, only afterwards asking, "Why?"

"And then you hold on to something, or to someone else that is holding on to something. I want to take a look out over the side, and I don't want to go for a swan dive if the ship suddenly chooses that moment to start dancing again."

Once they had a short human chain set up, Quinne went to look out over the side. Although it hadn't seemed like it in their hurry to get higher, they had gone up about six or seven stories. Some distance below her she could see the main walkway of the deck that went all the way around the ship, with several more stories beyond that before the water. At least, that was the way it was supposed to be. The *Lucky Lady Duck* was clearly still at a slight tilt, with their opposite side farther down in the water and this side elevated. Whatever had happened to cause the ship to start tilting, it probably wouldn't take that much more for the whole cruise ship to go completely over onto its side. Quinne remembered seeing that happen to another ship on the news quite a few years back, yet it had never occurred to her that it would happen to the boat she might be on. She guessed she'd just assumed that safety precautions had been taken since then to make sure something like it never happened again. Those precautions probably would have worked if not for, surprise surprise, an attack by three aquatic dinosaurs.

"See anything interesting?" Jimmy asked from his spot as the anchor of the human chain.

"Interesting, yes. Comforting, no. The tilt is worse than I thought it would be."

"That's nice and all, but what about the sea monsters?" Wanda asked. "Anything?"

Now that Wanda mentioned it, Quinne couldn't see any sign of the three creatures. And given how active they had been such a short time ago, she couldn't help but think that had to mean something bad. She said as much out loud, but Wanda scoffed.

"Since when is the lack of murderous sea creatures such a bad thing?" Wanda asked.

In a few seconds they had their answer. It wasn't an answer anyone could have possibly predicted.

That sound came again, the mournful, horrible wail, and this time it lasted for several seconds longer than either of the other times. If there had been time, Quinne probably would have quipped something about how Wanda had just had to say something, didn't she, but no sooner had the words occurred to her that there was another sound, along with a slight shake of the ship. The sound was obviously some kind of splash, very similar to when the liopleurodon had jumped from the water to take Sarah, and yet, despite being farther away, it could be heard more clearly. Half a second of thought told Quinne that this must be because something new had come out of the water, something bigger. She saw something flying toward them, something that made zero sense, and if her brain had paused for just a breath longer to try to identify it, all four of them would have died in that very instant. Instead her instincts took over, telling her to run before she could even understand what was happening, and the other three followed her, all of them desperately going full speed down the walkway, trying to avoid the massive shape coming toward them, getting bigger, more improbable, more ridiculous, and yet no less deadly.

Then the place where they had just been standing was hit with a liopleurodon.

No, not just *a* liopleurodon, Quinne corrected herself as the concussion from the force of the hit behind them threw them all off their feet. *The* liopleurodon. There was only supposed to be one, according to everything they had seen so far, and it definitely wasn't supposed to be flying. And as it smashed sidelong into the ship, obliterating the walkway and rooms both behind them as well as anyone or anything that might have been on the floors directly above or below them, Quinne understood it hadn't been flying at all.

It hit like an explosion, and as Quinne found herself twisting in the air from the force of the hit, facing backwards as she flew away from the impact. She saw as the liopleurodon, its head directly facing them, made one final desperate attempt to snap at them, as if it personally blamed them somehow for its predicament and wanted one last half-hearted attempt at revenge. Debris rained around her as she hit the floorboards. Quinne tucked herself into a protective ball, taking special care to shield her eyes. Something hit her hard on her broken arm, and while she did manage to keep from screaming, she thought she might have blacked out for a few more seconds at the pain. Whatever had hit her was big and hard and heavy. As she sat there on the floor, her body wracked with pain, chaos falling all around her, her eyes shut tight against any small flying objects threatening to blind her, the thought occurred to her that she could give up here. Really, she'd done well, considering. She was happy enough with what she had done with her life, and she'd done far more than was expected of her to keep that life over the last several hours when her vacation had become Hell. If she was done now and she opened her eyes to find herself in some Great Beyond she hadn't fully believed in before, she would be at peace with that. Right?

Right?

No. Not right. Fuck giving up. She hadn't given up through the various traumas of her past, so she sure as shit wasn't going to give up now. Time to open her eyes, assess herself, and see what she could do about squeaking a few more minutes out of her life.

She moaned and shoved away something that had landed on her, something that didn't want to budge. Once she realized it was one of the planters she'd seen earlier, she stopped trying to push it and instead just rolled it off on its side. The way it had landed resulted in a lot of pressure and pain in her ankle, but it wasn't nearly the agony of her broken arm. She'd probably still be able to stand on her ankle and run if she had to, although it would not be pleasant.

Sitting up and looking at the ruin around her, it was difficult to make sense of the state of things. Farther down the walkway everything looked fine, if a little toppled and disheveled from the impact. Quinne seemed to be in transitionary zone of destruction, where the floor was broken and hanging badly in some areas, but most of the mess was broken pieces and parts from where the liopleurodon hit.

And that was the weirdest sight of all. It had created a sort of impact crater in the side of the ship. As far as she could tell, it was a more or less round area of destruction a couple of stories high and wide, although she couldn't be sure from her current perspective. The liopleurodon was in the center of it all, apparently impaled on support beams and other pieces of shredded cruise ship. She could see jagged chunks of metal protruding from its hide in some places and keeping its dying form from slipping back into the ocean. It had other wounds as well, the likely results of its fighting with the other creatures, yet still, with all this damage, it appeared to be hanging on to its last shreds of life. Its head turned away to the sea and it made a mournful hooting noise as it wiggled, trying to dislodge itself.

It looked exactly like one of those old singing wall-mounted fish. Despite her anger, despite her pain, despite her fear, Quinne laughed.

"And that's why I'm going to hell," Quinne muttered. Finally, it occurred to her that she was the only person she could see, and began frantically looking around for the others. It didn't seem possible that all four of them could have somehow survived this, yet she quickly found her three companions in various piles of debris. Wanda looked like she had suffered the least. The impact had somehow thrown her the farthest down the walkway, and the worst she could claim was she'd fallen in a painfully awkward way when she hit. Amani looked the worst at first glance, but a quick check and a speedy use of some of the first aid supplies they'd found revealed that while she was cut up in a great many places, none of the shrapnel had hit anything vital and most of her wounds were superficial.

When they pulled Jimmy out from under a broken door, though, they saw the worst damage in their particular group.

"Something's wrong," Jimmy muttered. "Something wrong with my eye. Why can't I see?"

"You can't see at all?" Quinne asked.

"I… I guess I can see with my right eye. It's foggy, but there. Why can't I see with my left?"

He couldn't see with his left eye because he didn't have one anymore. The socket was actually empty, with a few nasty trailing cords of viscera from which it probably should have been hanging. They would probably even be able to find it somewhere in the pile if they took the time to look for it. But Quinne was pretty sure their time was almost up. Instead Wanda gently cooed soothing things to him while Quinne and Amani did their best to create makeshift bandages from pieces of their clothing. The binding job they did over his gaping hole probably wasn't very good, but Jimmy was the nurse, not any of them, and he was too shocked to give them any pointers.

"Is it dead?" Amani asked, pointing back in the direction of the liopleurodon. It wasn't moving anymore.

"Looks like it to me," Quinne said.

They had to hurry away from it as the floorboards beneath their feet strained. Too much more time here and the floor would probably give out from under them. But as for where exactly they should go, Quinne was at a loss. The entire ship was still rocking from the creature's impact, and while that had somehow tilted it slightly back from it precarious position, she had no doubt that the resulting loss of structurally integrity to the *Lucky Lady Duck* meant that it was probably sinking faster now.

"I don't get it," Wanda said as they stopped near the end of the walkway, both to catch their breaths and because they had nowhere else to go. "Why would it do that?"

"Why would what do what?" Quinne asked.

"The leo plural... thing. Why would it just jump at the ship like that and kill itself?"

"And why were they all fighting to begin with?" Jimmy asked, his voice ragged and hoarse. "None of them seemed to have a problem with each other earlier in the night."

Quinne was pretty sure she'd figured out the answer, but to her surprise Amani answered first. "It didn't jump at the ship. They were fighting because something agitated them. Whatever's been making that noise, I think they're scared of it. They were fighting probably out of confusion or something."

"What the hell could possibly be so scary that it frightens three huge sea monsters?" Jimmy asked.

"So, what, the leo thing jumped at the ship in some desperate attempt to get away?" Wanda asked.

"No, not jumped," Quinne said. "If it had done that under its own power, it would have come at the ship head on. It didn't. It hit the ship on its side."

"Meaning what?" Jimmy asked.

"Meaning something threw it," Amani said. "Something out there in the water picked up the giant prehistoric sea creature and threw it at us."

There were several moments of silence before both Wanda and Jimmy started cussing. "So we're screwed," Jimmy finally said. "That's it. No trying to swim away, no lifeboats, no anything is going to protect us from something like that."

"Things can't get much worse," Wanda said.

"Honey, I know you mean well, but please tell me you didn't just say that," Jimmy said. "Every single time anyone ever says that things can't get worse, that's exactly when things get worse."

"I know that, but I did it on purpose," Wanda said. "I figure that's such a horrible cliché, that this time, instead of things getting worse, something will suddenly happen to make things better."

Quinne shook her head. "Sorry, Wanda, but I'm pretty sure that's never, ever the way things work out."

That was when they heard the sound of approaching helicopters.

# CHAPTER FIFTEEN

"Honey, if you weren't standing on my left side where I can't see you, I'd kiss you," Jimmy said.

"If you save it for later we might be able to do more," Wanda said.

"Which direction is the sound coming from?" Quinne asked.

"Um, Quinne?" Amani said. "We're in the Arctic Circle. There pretty much isn't anywhere for something to come from except south."

"Um, right. How about which direction relative to the ship?"

"Sounds like the front to me," Wanda said.

"We need to get higher," Quinne said. "If we can't even see them, they sure won't be able to see us."

The sounds had been faint at first, enough that Quinne thought they might just be wishful thinking, but they were definitely noticeable now. And their group wasn't the only ones who had heard them. From somewhere below them, they could hear a large crowd of people, likely on the front deck, cheer at the approaching rescue. Quinne suspected this wasn't going to be an immediate happy ever after, however. According to Masterson and his people, there were only going to be three choppers, at least in the first wave. And given what had happened with the liopleurodon, Quinne didn't think the *Lucky Lady Duck* would still be here when the second wave arrived.

"It looks like there's another set of stairs over here," Amani said, gesturing down an interior hall. With Quinne using Amani to help support her weight and Jimmy using Wanda to guide him, the foursome found their way to the stairs and went up the last couple of flights to reach the very top of the ship. Here the wide open space was taken up with, of all the goddamned things, a golf course. Quinne could just imagine wild golf balls getting caught in the wind to fly deep out in the Arctic, where they would bean some unfortunate polar bear in the head. There had to be environmental regulations about that sort of thing, not that the Letroix Corporation would always see fit to follow such rules when they were so far from civilization.

"This is surreal," Amani said as they all came out onto the golf course. "We're on a golf course up about ten stories in the Arctic Ocean while we wait for helicopters to rescue us from sea monsters."

"Hon, please don't say something like 'it can't get any stranger than this,'" Quinne said.

"Oh h… er, fuck no," Amani said. "Wouldn't dream of it."

"Look! They're over there!" Wanda pointed out to some distant point near the horizon. Quinne's heart nearly stopped with her relief at the sight. She didn't know enough about helicopters to be able to identify the make by name, but they were the kind with twin rotors on top, as well as open sides. Their emergency-red color made them easy to see even from a distance. That also made it clear that instead of the promised three, there were five.

"Oh thank God," Wanda said. Quinne saved the thanking, though. Sure, five was better than three. But there were hundreds or thousands of people still on this ship. Five wasn't enough. The percentage of people who survived was going to be very, very small, and just because their group was at the highest point didn't mean that they were the first ones the choppers would go for. The cheers from the deck meant the number of people who had gathered there would be massive, making that a highly likely target for the helicopters' first stop.

They weren't the only ones who had worked their way to the top of the ship, though. At the end of the golf course closest to the front, there was already a small crowd of others that had gathered. Quinne could certainly be a vindictive person under the right circumstances, but she was still disturbed by her anger and disappointment in seeing that Lundgren was among them. And of course, where there was Lundgren there was also Masterson, his two cronies, and the chick that Masterson had picked as his love interest for this particular adventure.

"Does it make me a bad person that I'm disappointed to see they're still alive?" Amani quietly asked Quinne as they made their way across the golf course.

"If you're a bad girl, then I'm a bad girl, Amani. Don't worry about it."

"Wait, didn't you literally do a series called *I'm a Bad Girl*?" Jimmy asked Quinne.

"Should I be upset that you know that?" Wanda asked.

"Only if I watch it without you."

"Wow, lots of flirting," Quinne said. "Do remember that they probably won't let you two jump each other's bones in the helicopter."

A shadow crossed over Wanda's face. She gestured with her head at Quinne. Taking the hint, Quinne had Amani take over helping Jimmy while Quinne and Wanda hung back a little, the two of them engaging in a low conversation.

"I think I already know what you're going to say," Quinne said.

"Do you? And what am I going to say?"

"Something to the effect of, if it comes between making sure you get out of here or Jimmy instead, make sure it's Jimmy. Am I right?"

"More or less."

"You really don't value yourself that much?"

"I value myself quite a bit. But I'm dead in a few months anyway. I shouldn't be taking a spot on that helicopter that can go to someone else."

"So what are you going to do, just walk away when the helicopters come? Jimmy's not going to let that happen."

"Then you need to hold Jimmy back. He still has time left. Lots of it. I know he loves me, but I also don't think he would have really married me if the situation were different. At least, not yet. He might have later, but not now. When I'm gone, he can still live and find another."

"You know this is cliché as shit, right?"

"Do you promise me you'll do what you can to make sure he doesn't stay behind with me?"

"What if you don't have to stay behind? What if the helicopters come back in time to get you as well? You're not going to do something stupid like jump off the side of the ship once he's gone, are you?"

"I love my life. If I see a way to get those last few months, then I'm taking it. I'm not going to be throwing anything away. But come on now, Quinne. Be serious. We both know there isn't going to be anything left for a second wave of the rescue to get. Right?"

Quinne nodded grimly. "Fine. I'll do what I can. But I'm hardly in a state to stop him if he goes charging after you."

"That's all I ask."

Masterson and the rest of the group at the edge of the golf course were so busy waving their hands in an attempt to get the attention of the helicopters that none of them paid any attention as Quinne, Amani, and the newlyweds joined them. Lundgren noticed their presence after a few seconds and gave Quinne the stink eye, but otherwise he said nothing. There was a palpable sense of relief among the group that disturbed Quinne a bit. They were absolutely, one hundred percent sure that they were the ones the helicopters would come for first. There was no way it could be any different. Quinne looked down at the front deck of the ship and saw every other survivor of the ship down there, and she wondered if any of them had the same level of certainty. Or maybe some of them saw the number of helicopters and understood. There were certain people who always got rescued first while others were left for later. This was the way of things. The fact that the pansexual porn star, the young Muslim woman, and the black couple were up here with the so-called important ones was pure luck. Looking down at all those people, the vast majority of which she knew very well were never going to make it off, made Quinne want to throw up.

Masterson and his own people didn't seem to have these same troubled thoughts, but neither did they look as celebratory as those around them. Masterson may have proved himself to be little more than a moron masquerading as an intellectual, but he seemed to at least have the sense to know that this wasn't over yet. While Gordon and Mickey nervously gave exposition regarding the approaching rescue, Masterson lifted his assault rifle and...

Wait, what?

"Where the hell did Masterson get an assault rifle?" Quinne asked. Her question wasn't directed at anyone in particular, but Lundgren was the one who gave her an answer.

"Found it in the emergency supplies," Lundgren said simply.

"Since when the flying fuck does a family cruise ship need an assault rifle in its emergency stocks?" Quinne asked.

"Look, don't go asking me for the logic," Lundgren said. "Masterson didn't seem so surprised to find it, though. It's like he just kind of assumed it was his right and fate to have it."

"You're head of security. You didn't try to take it away from him?"

"Why would I?"

"If I or Amani or Jimmy had walked up here carrying an

assault rifle, what would you have done?"

"I would have shot your asses." Lundgren didn't seem to think there was anything hypocritical about any of this, and Quinne figured it wasn't an argument she would win. It was hard to argue with people who refused to use logic.

A spontaneous cheer erupted from the massive crowd below, although Quinne wasn't quite sure what exactly had triggered it. In response, though, that noise came again. Mournful. Sorrowful. Alien. Ungodly loud. So loud, in fact, that that every single person below went quiet as they had to cover their ears. Quinne and everyone on the golf course followed suit. She didn't even have to wait for the sound, so much longer than any of the times before, to be finished before she understood exactly what it meant.

Time was up. This was the end.

# CHAPTER SIXTEEN

From their spot at the top of the ship, Quinne had the perfect view of the horror show that happened next. The first thing she saw was the plesiosaurus some distance off to the right side, but she saw immediately that something was wrong with it. Instead of rising to the surface head-first, she saw its tail and backside bob up. Even from this distance she could see that the plesiosaurus had taken substantial damage from its fights, and not every wound could be accounted for by just the megalodon and the liopleurodon. In fact, there was one very noticeable wound along its side that had clearly not been the result of teeth but of some long, straight, sharp object, like a knight had gone up to the creature and tried to slay it with a sword, getting in a mortal wound before the plesiosaurus got its revenge. The gouge was so bad that Quinne couldn't begin to understand how it could still be alive, and yet it bogged and thrashed organically, like it was in the final struggle of its life. She didn't think anyone else noticed this. Most of the people's attention was once more on the helicopters as they came within rescuing distance. They probably would have been able to load the most people if they had been able to land, but passengers had taken up every available flat space on the deck. While four of the helicopters hovered, their pilots obviously taking a moment to assess the situation, the fifth helicopter broke away from the others.

It headed for the top of the ship, the golf course, and the people waiting there.

"Everyone, make room!" Masterson extrapolated. "Give the chopper some place to land!" Not that anyone really had to move anywhere. There were plenty of flat open spaces behind them. Masterson seemed to be giving orders purely because he thought he had to.

"It's coming!" Amani said. "Quinne, we're actually going to make it out of here!"

Quinne heard her but paid little attention. The plesiosaurus vanished back into the water like it had been sucked down.

When it came back up, though…

The thing that held the plesiosaur by the neck looked very much like a tentacle, but not so much the tentacle of an octopus or squid. It was chitinous, like an insect, and segmented, reminding Quinne of the close-up view of a spider's leg, except with infinitely more joints. And unlike a spider, it wasn't black or brown or red. Instead the tentacle was translucent, the muscles and nerve endings and other unidentifiable interior structures visible through a gauzy haze. In that way it reminded Quinne of some kind of tapeworm, or perhaps some sort of exotic jellyfish. Of course, Quinne had never seen a tapeworm or jellyfish tentacle that was nearly ten stories long, so that comparison ultimately failed.

In the end, there wasn't actually much of anything Quinne could compare it with. This was not another prehistoric sea creature. There would be no finding this thing in the fossil record. No matter what that tentacle might be attached to beneath the water, it was something that no human had seen before.

"Holy…!" Masterson expatriated. That was the only sound anyone was able to make before the tentacle whipped the dead or dying plesiosaurus back and, using it like a club, slammed it down on the front deck of the *Lucky Lady Duck*. No one on the deck had time to scatter, and even if they had had the time, they were packed so closely together they wouldn't have been able to run anyway. The bulk of the plesiosaurus crushed a huge number of people all at once, creating a massive spurt of red like someone had crushed a blood-filled water balloon with a sledgehammer. Quinne screamed, and one of the children with one of the other people on the golf course cried, but the carnage was too quick to otherwise react. The tentacle lifted the dead and broken monster again, and this time when in attacked the plesiosaurus came down at an angle, not just smashing more innocent passengers but also sweeping a large number of them off the side.

The helicopter over the golf course stopped its descent, obviously deciding that actually landing was too risky when something completely terrible and unknown was happening below. The other helicopters started to pull up and away, but before they could make a safe distance two more of the tentacles erupted up from the other side of the ship. One grabbed a helicopter through the open door in its side while the other tentacle tried to wrap itself completely around a different helicopter. The rotors sliced large chunks out of the tentacle, causing the tentacle to retract all the way back into the water, but the tentacle had still managed to damage the chopper's back rotor. It started spinning out of control and hit the water with a colossal splash. The first tentacle again smashed the increasingly broken plesiosaurus against the deck. Although the cruise ship had shaken with every impact so far, this time Quinne could tell that the damage was critical. The *Lucky Lady Duck* lurched beneath them all, tilting forward as the front end of the ship slipped beneath the water. Quinne no longer had any time to be horrified for the thousands of people dying below them. She was too busy trying not to slide right over the edge of the golf course.

Gordon slipped, hit a protective railing that was supposed to keep people from falling off the roof of the ship, and then tumbled off below.

"Gordon?" Masterson asked. Actually asked instead of whatever the hell else he had been doing. He seemed thoroughly confused about what had just happened. "That's… that's not the way he's supposed to die. He's supposed to have the final heroic sacrifice that saves the rest of us. I don't…"

Quinne didn't pay attention to anything else he said. Instead she hit the ground and grabbed at the artificial turf of the last hole's putting green. "Down!" Quinne yelled at her friends. "The lower you are, the less likely you'll lose your balance and fall!" This left her unable to see what was happening below them, but from the way the ship rocked and shifted she could tell this was it. This was the moment the *Lucky Lady Duck* finally sank. And it wasn't going to be like in *Titanic* either, something that inexorably took up screen time. She could see more tentacles just over the edge of the roof, coming up and then dashing down to dig into the ship. This thing, this final boss sea monster, wasn't going to wait for the ship to sink under its own power. It was going to pull the ship down.

Amani followed her lead, but found a better hand hold in the last hole itself. Neither Jimmy nor Wanda looked like they were able to grab on to anything, but the angle of the ship wasn't quite enough yet for their weight to overcome their friction against the turf. Quinne looked back at the others and saw a teenage girl of about fifteen, looking frightened and unsure as she fell and tumbled toward the edge. She stopped herself right before the railing, but not before bowling into Mickey, who in turn hit Masterson's fuckbuddy and sent them both toppling against side railing.

"Mickey? You're supposed to give the final quip," Masterson said. "And Nina, what about our final kiss? This isn't the way these stories are supposed to go. I'm the hero." He stumbled toward the edge, yet managed to keep his footing.

"I hate to break it to you, Masterson," Quinne called at him, "but I don't think you were ever the hero of this story. Real stories like this don't have heroes. The best they get is survivors."

"I'm the hero!" Masterson screamed at the sky. He didn't give any more indication that Quinne existed than he had during any of the rest of this trip. "I'm supposed to save the day! I even have an assault rifle! That's how it works! I'm…"

A huge tentacle snaked over the edge, wrapped itself around him, and then yanked him away. The last scream he made was high-pitched until it cut off abruptly.

Quinne looked up at the rescue helicopter, which was managing to stay just out of range of any of the tentacles. The pilot had apparently abandoned any thought of landing or getting closer, but a metal basket lowered from its side, moving down in their direction. Quinne looked around for everyone that hadn't fallen, only to be shocked that, out of the entire group that had been here, only six remained. Other than Quinne's group, the only people that had managed not to fall were Lundgren and the teenage girl, and she was just barely holding on.

"Lundgren, you've got to get her!" Quinne screamed.

For several seconds it looked like Lundgren was going to ignore her. Quinne could have tried to help the girl, but Lundgren was closer, and he didn't have the disadvantage of a broken arm or sprained ankle.

*Come on, Lundgren, do the right thing*, Quinne thought. There had to be a part of him that wasn't a selfish bastard. He hesitated as the ship lurched, everything underneath them dropping a few feet. Finally, as Lundgren caught his balance, a pained look came over his face. He looked at Quinne and the others, scowled, and then went back for the girl. While Quinne and the others struggled to help each other, Lundgren grabbed the girl by the hand and yanked her in the direction of the rescue basket. If the ship hadn't dropped, the basket would have been low enough to rest on the golf course by now. Instead it was a few feet in the air, and Lundgren had to lift the girl up and shove her over the side to get her in. He then grabbed a hold and pulled himself in with her, then turned to the others and held out his hand.

"Move!" he yelled. His cry was drowned out by the creaking and screeching of metal. While the back end of the *Lucky Lady Duck* had previously been slowly rising up as the tentacles grabbed the ship and tried to pull it under, the back now shifted so that the ground beneath them was almost even. That might have seemed like a good thing under other circumstances, but here it could only mean that the tentacles must have grabbed the other end of the ship as well and were pulling it down to join the front. The basket appeared to shoot up out of the reach of Quinne and the others, and then slowly continued to rise.

"What's happening?" Amani asked. "Why are they flying away?"

"They're not flying away," Wanda said. "We're sinking faster."

Whoever was at the controls of the helicopter was reeling in the basket with Lundgren and the girl, but from the other side they were lowering another basket. It was dropping as fast as it could go, but the downward momentum of the sinking ship was faster. The helicopter tried to compensate by lowering with it, but now tentacles whipped every which way, a few of them coming very close to the rotors.

"Amani, jump for the basket!" Quinne screamed at her. The young woman didn't hesitate, leaping for the basket right as it got within reach and getting a good grip on the edge. She pulled herself up and over, then turned to help the others.

"Come on! You can do it!" Amani yelled at her. The ship kept dropping, and the helicopter wasn't lowering itself anymore for fear of the tentacles. This was it. The last chance for all of them.

Quinne spared only the briefest of glances at Jimmy and Wanda, just enough to see that both of them were about to try the jump as well, before she jumped for the basket. Her right arm hit the side, causing enough pain that she had to desperately fight to keep consciousness, but she got her left arm high enough to hook over the edge of the basket, where Amani grabbed onto her and did her best to keep Quinne from falling. Keeping hold became so much harder less than a second later, though, when she felt a weight grip her bad ankle and yank downward. At first she thought one of the tentacles had to have gotten her, until she looked down and saw Jimmy clinging to her leg for dear life with one arm while he offered the other to Wanda, who grabbed on just as the ship shifted again to drop dramatically below her.

"We've got everyone!" Amani yelled up at the helicopter. "Go up! Up, up, up, up!"

Quinne knew the last thing she probably wanted to do in this situation was look down, yet she couldn't help herself. The helicopter jerked upward, a move that would have caused Quinne to lose her grip if Amani weren't hold her so hard that the young woman's fingernails tore up Quinne's arm. The view below them was breathtaking, and amazing, and horrible, and a thing out of nightmares. Tentacles now swarmed every part of the *Lucky Lady Duck*, and the ship sank below the water faster than it had any right to.

As the helicopter went higher and higher, desperate to get out of the way of the few tentacles still trying to grasp for it, Quinne's view of the chaos and destruction became more complete. Huge sections of the ship had been broken off or else pulled off, and many translucent tentacles grasped for each piece, greedily yanking them down into the deep blue. There were still some people down there, tiny thrashing specks in the water, but many of those vanished as Quinne watched, sucked down by something no one could see. Up, and up, and up, and now Quinne could see the shades of darkness in the water, a slowly expanding round patch of shadow showing that something was under there, something massive, something that had somehow become bigger than the ship it was swallowing up and still even appeared to be growing.

As much as the curiosity taunted her, Quinne decided she most definitely did not want to see what created that dark blue blob in the Arctic Ocean. If she did, she didn't think she would ever be able to sleep again.

The helicopter kept rising. The winch controlling the basket whined as it slowly raised them up. Below them, all signs that there had ever been a cruise ship here, along with untold numbers of families, workers, and various vacationers, completely vanished into the deep.

"I'm not sure how much longer I can hold on," Quinne said to Amani, trying to keep her voice at a volume that only the young woman would have been able to hear. It was difficult, though, trying to still be heard over the buzz of the helicopter rotors, and Wanda and Jimmy must have been able to hear.

"Jimmy, I just want you to know that the brief time we were married was the happiest in my life," Wanda said. "I love... Ow! What are you doing?"

"I'm tightening my grip so you don't do something stupid like let go thinking that less weight will somehow save us. Did you honestly think I didn't know you were going to try something like this? I've changed your bedpans, honey. I know you far better than you think."

"Jimmy, please. I'm as good as dead anyways. Don't sacrifice yourself just for..."

"Stuff it, Wanda. You didn't think I married you just out of pity, did you? I love you, and I'm not going to give up any of my time with you. Period."

"Very romantic," Quinne said through clenched teeth. "But I still don't know how long I..."

The sea erupted below them. Quinne looked down to see the megalodon jumping out of the water. She could see immediately, with the perfect clarity that is supposed to happen in the moment before someone dies and their life flashes before their eyes, that with its mouth wide open like that, and given its speed and size, that it would get them. At the very least it would snap Wanda, Jimmy, and Quinne out of the air. Quinne's eyes went up to Amani, and they exchanged a look that was both terrified and meaningful. Amani was probably about to die as well, and possibly everyone on the helicopter, if the megalodon had just the right amount of height. Quinne wished she had the time to tell Amani how good it had been to spend her last hours with the young woman, that, while there obviously hadn't been the time to fall in love or anything silly and romantic like that, that Quinne still cared, that if they had lived she would do what she could to help Amani come to terms with her sexuality, that their time on the doomed cruise ship would not have been the end. And Quinne thought she could see something similar in the way Amani looked back at her.

Quinne closed her eyes, waiting for the megalodon to snap its jaws shut around her.

"Holy fucking shitballs!" Amani yelled.

Quinne opened her eyes and looked down again just in time to see a final mass of tentacles whip up into the air. They were fast, faster than Quinne could have possibly imagined, and they grabbed for any last morsels they could get. They were probably long enough that they could have snatched the three hanging from the basket with no problem. But instead there was something in their way, something bigger, something more filling. The tentacles snapped around the megalodon, constricting so fast and tight that they managed to squeeze off the creature's massive dorsal fin, which separated from the megalodon in a shower of blood and fell back to the water.

Before the fin could hit, the ocean beneath it opened up.

Everything happened so quick, less than a second, that Quinne would spend the rest of her life debating what exactly it was she saw. All she would have were fractured memories and images.

There was a whirlpool, a vacuum opening in the middle of the sea. There was something in the middle, something dark, something throbbing. There were long white things, possibly teeth.

She wouldn't be able to put all these shards of memory together until later, when she would come to the conclusion that the enormous, gaping hole in the ocean had to be a mouth, the mouth of something so large, and possibly still pulsing with growth, that the human mind didn't have the proper context to fully understand.

The tentacles yanked. The megalodon fell back down before it could get its final meal, and disappeared as the waters crashed back down to cover the brief glimpse of the thing that had been hiding below the Arctic Ocean.

And when the waters were calm again, the massive bulk of the black shadow under the sea was gone.

# CHAPTER SEVENTEEN

"Quinne? Quinne! Come on back. You're drifting from us again."

Quinne blinked, only now realizing that she was in the helicopter. "Huh?"

She looked around at the interior of the helicopter. Someone was closing the doors, so Quinne assumed there wasn't going to be any more attempts at rescues. Strangely, it looked like she had spaced out during the rescue of some other people: in addition to Amani, Wanda, Jimmy, Lundgren, and the teen girl, there were three more passengers, all of them dripping wet and huddled under blankets. In addition to the survivors there were two men and one woman that were obviously part of the rescue crew, as well as a pilot and co-pilot in the front. Given the size of the helicopter, it was sobering to see how much of the space was free rather than crammed full of passengers of the doomed *Lucky Lady Duck*. The only good thing about this was that the few survivors were able to get food, blankets, and medical attention immediately.

The female rescue worker was in the process of looking over Quinne's arm and praising Jimmy for the job he'd done on it under the circumstances. Amani was on her other side holding Quinne's hand. Quinne squeezed it, and Amani squeezed back.

"What happened?" Quinne asked. "Did I pass out?"

"It looked like you were still conscious," Jimmy said. The makeshift bandage over his missing eye had been replaced by something sturdier and more sanitary, but that didn't make him look any less rough. Wanda was asleep and snoring gently beside him. Quinne couldn't blame her. Her body, such as it was, had probably been working harder to keep her going than any of theirs had. "Your mind just took a little break, is all. Wolfe over there didn't seem too concerned as long as you came out of it at some point." He pointed at the female rescue worker, who nodded at Quinne in response. When Wolfe moved off to check on the teenager, Amani leaned over and whispered in Quinne's ear.

"By the way, she's probably too much of a professional to say anything, but given the way Wolfe looked at you when she pulled us in, I think she might be a fan of yours. Or, at the very least, she recognized you."

Quinne made a mental note to give the woman an autograph at some point as a show of appreciation, provided she could bring it up in such a way that wouldn't make Wolfe feel awkward.

*Holy shit, what the hell am I even thinking? Now is not the time to think about giving autographs*, Quinne thought. Or maybe it was. Maybe her brain desperately needed to latch onto something normal, or at least as normal one could get when it came to the idea of signing naked pictures of oneself. All of these people here, rescue crew included, had been through something horrendous.

"The other rescue helicopters," Quinne said. "What about them?"

Amani shook her head sadly. "I overheard some of the chatter from the pilots," she said quietly so the rescue workers wouldn't hear. "Of the five choppers, two went down. The pilot of one was recovered, but everybody else on those two…"

"Gone," Quinne whispered. Amani nodded. Gone just like thousands of people who had simply wanted to go on a fun, out of the way vacation. Just disappeared into the icy waters, and no real explanation for any of it. Would any of this ever get explained, Quinne wondered, or would the sudden appearance of three prehistoric monsters and one, well, one something else just become a mystery that would haunt people for generations, like the disappearance of the Roanoke colony or the unknown fate of the crew of the *Mary Celeste*? Hell, would anyone even believe any of the survivors at all when they told stories of what had come out of the ocean that night? Would there be any proof, or would late-night pundits just try saying that the survivors suffered from some kind of group hallucination?

"Two other helicopters," Quinne said in hushed tones. "Did anyone else get rescued?"

"One helicopter found two more people," Amani said. "The other was going out to check on something they thought they saw. The pilots are spooked, obviously, but they're going back out anyway. Apparently there's more on the way, but no actual ships will come within a certain radius."

"They'll probably declare the area a radiation zone or something, some kind of waste spill or something else like that they can use to cover it up," Jimmy said. "I highly doubt any of this incident is ever going to get looked into. At least not by anyone that doesn't wear a black suit, sunglasses, and report to a government agency without a name."

"So that's it," Quinne said. "Us in here, two others, and whoever they might find still floating out there. Out of everyone." She thought about Becky, the girl in the Lucky Lady Duck suit, and Sarah, the woman who had asked for Bobby in her final moments. She thought of the boy who had been reading in the hall during the first attack. Hell, she even thought of the asshole in the red trucker's cap. He would be dead, too, and he deserved it just as little as anyone else had. People might try to tell stories about what had happened here. News organizations would interview the few survivors repeatedly. Shit, someone would probably get a book deal out of it, although Quinne already swore that wouldn't be her. Everyone who hadn't been here would try to find someone to act as the hero that Masterson had so desperately wanted to be. But there were no heroes in situations like this. Just some people who happened to live, and many, many more who hadn't.

While Quinne would have normally thought that the insides of helicopters would be too loud to hear anything, these apparently had something in them to cancel the noise, all owing Quinne to hear talk from the co-pilot about the last helicopter out looking for someone. There were two objects in the water, apparently. Quinne hoped that, whomever it was, they were still alive.

"And any more sign of that… that thing?" Quinne asked.

"It seems to be gone," Amani said. "No sign of it. Just vanished as mysteriously as it appeared. The rescue people still don't want to take any extra chances, though."

Quinne wanted to ask what would happen to all of them now, but that would be a waste of breath. That answer could only come in time. How Jimmy would live with one eye, how much longer Wanda had, whether Amani would come to grips with herself and her family, even what Quinne did from here—there were never any easy answers. Quinne gripped Amani's hand, though, and then also lightly took Jimmy's in her damaged hand. Jimmy in turn took Wanda's. Four survivors that only still existed because they had found a way to do it all with someone else rather than alone.

"They've found something swimming in the water!" the co-pilot said. "But they don't think they're human."

Every one of the survivors of the *Lucky Lady Duck* tensed, certain that they were about to hear of yet another creature from the deep coming after them. When the co-pilot spoke again, though, they all relaxed.

"Uh, they say it looks like two huge rats."

# THE END

# CHECK OUT OTHER GREAT DEEP SEA THRILLERS

## PREHISTORIC BEASTS AND WHERE TO FIGHT THEM
by Hugo Navikov

IN THE DEPTHS, SOMETHING WAITS ...

Acclaimed film director Jake Bentneus pilots a custom submersible to the bottom of Challenger Deep in the Pacific, the deepest point of any ocean of Earth. But something lurks at the hot hydrothermal vents, a creature—a dinosaur—too big to exist.

Gigadon.

It not only exists, but it follows him, hungrily, back to the surface. Later, a barely living Bentneus offers a $1 billion prize to anyone who can find and kill the monster. His best bet is renowned ichthyopaleontologist Sean Muir, who had predicted adapted dinosaurs lived at the bottom of the ocean.

## MEGALODON: APEX PREDATOR
by S.J. Larsson

English adventurer Sir Jeffery Mallory charters a ship for a top secret expedition to Antarctica. What starts out as a search and capture mission soon turns into a terrifying fight for survival as the crew come face to face with the fiercest ocean predator to have ever existed- Carcharodon Megalodon. Alone and with no hope of rescue the crew will need all their resources if they are to survive not only a 60 foot shark but also the harsh Antarctic conditions. Megalodon: Apex Predator is a deep-sea adventure filled with action, twists and savage prehistoric sharks.

# CHECK OUT OTHER GREAT DEEP SEA THRILLERS

## HELL'S TEETH
by Paul Mannering

In the cold South Pacific waters off the coast of New Zealand, a team of divers and scientists are preparing for three days in a specially designed habitat 1300 feet below the surface.

In this alien and savage world, the mysterious great white sharks gather to hunt and to breed.

When the dive team's only link to the surface is destroyed, they find themselves in a desperate battle for survival. With the air running out, and no hope of rescue, they must use their wits to survive against sharks, each other, and a terrifying nightmare of legend.

## MONSTERS IN OUR WAKE
by J.H. Moncrieff

In the idyllic waters of the South Pacific lurks a dangerous and insatiable predator; a monster whose bloodlust and greed threatens the very survival of our planet...the oil industry. Thousands of miles from the nearest human settlement, deep on the ocean floor, ancient creatures have lived peacefully for millennia. But when an oil drill bursts through their lair, Nøkken attacks, damaging the drilling ship's engine and trapping the desperate crew. The longer the humans remain in Nøkken's territory, struggling to repair their ailing ship, the more confrontations occur between the two species. When the death toll rises, the crew turns on each other, and marine geologist Flora Duchovney realizes the scariest monsters aren't below the surface.

# CHECK OUT OTHER GREAT
# DEEP SEA THRILLERS

## LOCH NESS REVENGE
by Hunter Shea

Deep in the murky waters of Loch Ness, the creature known as Nessie has returned. Twins Natalie and Austin McQueen watched in horror as their parents were devoured by the world's most infamous lake monster. Two decades later, it's their turn to hunt the legend. But what lurks in the Loch is not what they expected. Nessie is devouring everything in and around the Loch, and it's not alone. Hell has come to the Scottish Highlands. In a fierce battle between man and monster, the world may never be the same. Praise for THEY RISE : "Outrageous, balls to the wall...made me yearn for 3D glasses and a tub of popcorn, extra butter!" – The Eyes of Madness "A fast-paced, gore-heavy splatter fest of sharksploitation." The Werd "A rocket paced horror story. I enjoyed the hell out of this book." Shotgun Logic Reviews

## TERROR FROM THE DEEP
by Alex Laybourne

When deep sea seismic activity cracks open a world hidden for millions of years, terrifying leviathans of the deep are unleashed to rampage off the coast of Mexico. Trapped on an island resort, MMA fighter Troy Deane leads a small group of survivors in the fight of their lives against pre-historic beasts long thought extinct. The terror from the deep has awoken, and it will take everything they have to conquer it.

www.ingramcontent.com/pod-product-compliance
Lightning Source LLC
Chambersburg PA
CBHW051955170626
46808CB00007B/2634